GOT THIS

CARA MAILEY & CHRISSIE SAINS

SCHOLASTIC

Published in the UK by Scholastic, 2022
Euston House, 24 Eversholt Street, London, NW1 1DB
Scholastic Ireland, 89E Lagan Road, Dublin Industrial Estate,
Glasnevin, Dublin, D11 HP5F

SCHOLASTIC and associated logos are trademarks and/or
registered trademarks of Scholastic Inc.

Text © Cara Mailey and Chrissie Sains, 2022

The right of Cara Mailey and Chrissie Sains to be identified
as the authors of this work has been asserted by them
under the Copyright, Designs and Patents Act 1988.

ISBN 978 0702 31498 8

A CIP catalogue record for this book
is available from the British Library.

Printed by CPI Group (UK) Ltd, Croydon, CR0 4YY
Papers used by Scholastic Children's Books are made
from wood grown in sustainable forests.

1 3 5 7 9 10 8 6 4 2

www.scholastic.co.uk

For Noah. Remember never to worry about our disability
– we can use it to inspire others. – CM

For Rich, Meg and Hattie. With love. – CS

CHAPTER 1

I can't believe that it's finally here.

The night that we've been counting down to *all* summer.

The most hotly anticipated concert in the whole of Belfast. A concert that sold out in twenty-two seconds! A concert that my mum actually managed to *win* tickets for.

Fusion; the greatest girl band on *earth*.

And here I am stuck in the toilet, trying to reach the lock with my left shoe.

"Is there anything that you can stand on?" My best friend, Aimee, peers down from the cubicle next door, her dark brown bob falling over her face as I raise my eyes towards her and sigh.

There's nothing. No stool. No bin. Not even a spare

bog roll, which, to be fair, would probably give me the extra four inches that I need.

We hear a really excited cheer from the arena.

"Do you think that's Fusion coming onstage?" Aimee turns towards the sound longingly as this amazing drumbeat pounds out. It gets faster and faster and faster until all of a sudden it stops, and everything goes quiet.

"*Good evening, Belfast!*" bursts out from the arena.

"I think it might be." I nod from the cubicle as we listen to the whole place erupting with excited screams.

So, how did I get stuck in the toilet at the most hotly anticipated concert of the year? Well, quite simply, I can't reach the bolt to unlock the door and get out.

Public toilets aren't exactly designed for someone my size.

I have achondroplasia, which is a type of dwarfism.

If I were to describe myself, I'd probably say small arms, small legs, *MASSIVE* Afro. Or sometimes I call myself a little person.

And yes, I know, how did I lock the door in the first place if I can't *unlock* it?

Well, let's just say that it turns out that *locking* a toilet door with a shoe is much easier than *unlocking* a toilet door with a shoe.

"I'll go back to our seats and get your dad." Aimee watches as I jump for the bolt the billionth time. "Or should I get your mum? Seeing as we're in the ladies' toilets. Or maybe your nan?" She tilts her head to one side as I stop jumping. It's tiring and it's *not* working. Mum won the tickets to tonight's concert, so my whole family are here, even my nan and my five-year-old little brother, Joe.

Mum and Joe have achondroplasia too, and Mum is always prepared for a *situation*.

She might not be able to stand on a toilet and poke her head over the cubicle to offer moral support, like Aimee can, but she'll know *exactly* what to do. Knowing her, she's probably put some kind of fold-up stool in Dad's rucksack, just in case.

"Talk to Mum first and see what she thinks," I reply. "And Aimee ... you don't need to come back with them. Stay and watch Fusion. There's no point in you missing it too."

"Don't be silly, Erin." Aimee meets my eyes. "I don't want to watch it without you."

Aimee's been my best friend since the first day of primary school. When we first met, most of the girls patted me on the head and called me cute, which might

3

sound like a nice thing to do, but believe me, when it happens at least ten times a day, it can get annoying. Aimee took one look at me, then turned away and carried on playing with the Lego.

I knew from that moment that she was the friend for me.

I ignored all the girls who were following me about, patting my head, and marched straight over to Aimee, plonked myself down next to her and started chatting.

Funnily enough, we're total opposites in most ways.

I'm short. Aimee is tall.

I'm outgoing and chatty. Aimee is shy and quiet.

I love cookie dough ice cream. Aimee loves lemon sorbet.

Mum says we're like chalk and cheese, but I think jam and cheese would be a better description, because even though you might not expect it, we're actually the perfect combination.

"Just stay there. I won't be long, OK?" Aimee's head disappears from above the cubicle and there's a rustling sound. "This is in case you get hungry." A mint humbug sails over the toilet door and plops into the toilet. "Oh." Aimee's head pokes back up as I shut the lid. "Sorry, that was my last one. I'll just go and get help." Her head ducks back down and I listen as the door opens and one of my favourite Fusion songs, "Love My Life", blasts into the room.

I clamber up on to the toilet lid to sit and wait as I wish for the billionth time that I just hadn't locked the door. But the toilets were busy when I first came in and I didn't want anyone to walk in on me. I know I should have just asked Aimee to wait outside, but I was feeling so good about tonight, and I *could* reach the lock with my shoe. What could possibly go wrong?

I give the bolt a death glare.

Being a little person has never bothered me, because, well, what's wrong with being little? It's just different, right? But it's not always easy to live in a world that's not exactly designed for me.

I listen to the concert from the comfort of my cubicle. At least I can still *hear* Fusion, even if I can't see them, and I start to sing along. I don't *normally* sing in the toilet, but Fusion sound properly *amazing* and before I know it, I'm belting out the words as if I were back at my seat watching them for real.

"Hello there?" a posh voice calls from outside the door. I've been so busy singing "Love My Life" at the top of my lungs, I didn't even hear anyone come in. "Are you *OK*?"

"Yes, I'm fine." I try to sound really reassuring, as if I always spend concerts stuck in toilets singing my heart out. "I'm locked in the toilet. My friend's gone for help."

"Oh," the person replies from outside the door. "Well, you sounded lovely in there. Beautiful voice."

"Thank you," I reply, feeling just a tad mortified.

"Are you a professional singer?" she asks conversationally as I hear her do a wee in the cubicle next to me.

"Errr ... no. Definitely not." I laugh awkwardly as I remember the last time that I tried to sing in front of an audience.

It did not go well.

I was seven years old, and I'd been picked to sing the very first solo in the school production. I was so excited. I love singing and dancing, and the idea of doing that in front of an audience... Well, that was my *dream*.

"Good luck," Isla Walsh, a girl in my class, whispered after me as I walked out on to the stage. "I'm sure everyone will love you..." She smiled sweetly as I reached the microphone. "No matter how you sing."

And that's when I hesitated. The thing with dwarfism is that you get stared at a *lot*. I guess people just can't get their heads around the fact that I look ... well, different.

But as I stood there in front of those parents, wanting them to look at me for a reason *other* than being small, hoping that instead of looking at my size, they'd listen to me sing and just maybe . . . they'd think that I was *good* at it.

Well, all of a sudden, that felt like an impossible dream.

I opened my mouth to sing and . . . nothing came out.

I looked out at the audience, a sea of faces watching me, and then I saw Mum. She was gripping hands with Nanny really tightly. Nodding at me. Willing me to sing. And for a moment, I thought, *Maybe I could do this*.

I took a deep breath, smiled, spread my arms wide, opened my mouth and—

Isla Walsh walked out on to the stage belting out *my* song.

I snapped my mouth shut again.

That was it.

My moment.

And I'd blown it.

CHAPTER 2

"Erin?" I hear my nanny's voice from outside the door. "Erin, are you OK?"

"Hi, Nanny," I call out as Aimee's head pokes up over the cubicle again. "Hi, Aimee." I grin.

"Fusion are *amazing*." Aimee peers down at me. "As soon as you're out of here, you're going to *love* this concert. And you'll have only missed the first couple of songs."

"Don't you worry, Erin," Nanny's reassuring voice rings out. "We'll have you out of there in a second..." She pushes something under the door.

It's a small folding step stool! I *knew* Mum would have brought something like this with us.

I get down from the toilet, unfold the stool, step on to it and unlock the door.

"Well, that's a relief," I hear the posh woman from outside saying. "I was just telling this young lady that she has a lovely singing— Oh." She stops talking as I walk out of the door, her eyes saucering. She looks *exactly* like she sounded: lipstick freshly applied and not a hair out of place. "Oh," she says again.

Unlike me, apparently.

Nanny blinks twice as we all stand there politely, not really knowing what to say next.

Most of the time, when people see me, they just smile, then look away and get on with whatever they're doing. But sometimes the reactions can be a bit more extreme.

Mum says to just ignore it and pretend not to notice, but of course I *do* notice. Secretly, I've put the reactions into four categories:

1. *The Smilers.* This is the most common. Total strangers who seem dead pleased to see me and who say things like, "Oh, aren't you small!" (in case I'd forgotten) or "Oh, you're so cute!" (ew). Sometimes, they even like to give me a friendly pat on the head (seriously?).

2. *The Not-So-Secret Glancers.* This group desperately want to stare, but they know that would be rude.

So instead, they talk to each other behind their hands and take secret peeks, while pretending not to.

Note to the Not-So-Secret Glancers: I can still see your eyes when your hand is in front of your mouth.

3. *The Starers.* Typically little kids, who just stop what they're doing and stare or point, with their mouths hanging open. This doesn't really bother me. I mean, they're just interested. I hate it when they get told off for it, or worse, dragged away. Better to just explain to them that everyone is different, don't you think?

4. *The Secret Photographers.* By far the most annoying group. This group pretends not to notice us at all. They just hold up their phones at a secret angle, making zero eye contact, trying to snap a photo of us.

Yep. It's properly weird. Just because I look different, they think they can take my picture without my permission? What do they want it for anyway? It's totally not OK.

Luckily my dad's like a sniffer dog when it comes to the secret photographers. He can spot them a mile away. The second he sees one, he saunters over really casually as if he hasn't noticed them *at all* (he has). Then he plonks himself between the camera and us, with his hands on his hips and a big dopey grin on his face, like he's actually kind of enjoying himself. It's really funny.

The lady in the toilets rearranges her face into a big fake smile. "Well, aren't you just so *cute*." She pats my head fondly. "Ooh." She rubs a strand of my Afro between her fingertips. "Your hair is so lovely."

"Err, thanks." I instinctively yank my head away from her. I've never really understood why people think it's OK to touch my hair like that, or to pat me on the head, come to think of it.

"Riiiiggghhht..." Nanny puts her hand protectively on my shoulder. "Well..." She gives the lady a polite but firm nod. "Bye then." She leads me out of the door.

The rest of the concert is properly *amazing*, and Aimee and I sing our hearts out to *every single song*.

"I know it didn't start well, but this is the best night *ever!*" Aimee squeezes my arm, just as Shani, Robin and Brooke walk to the front of the stage and stand there, really dramatically waiting for everyone to go quiet.

"Listen up, Belfast!" Shani calls out. "We have an

important announcement to make."

The whole arena goes *deathly* quiet.

"We have a really exciting opportunity coming up for anyone aged ten to fourteen!" Brooke is speaking now. "An opportunity to sing with us and to star in our next music video."

"No *way*!" Aimee grips my arm as there are literally hundreds of excited squeals from the audience.

"Our next hit is about us as kids." It's Robin's turn to talk now. "So, we're looking for three young fans to form Fusion Junior! If you can sing and dance and you've got a spark in your eye, like we had when we were your age, then we want to see your audition video."

"Erin!" Aimee bounces up and down in her seat in excitement. "You should do it!"

"Hey, it looks like someone here is very excited about this!" Shani bends down towards a girl waving her arms around near the stage. "Do you wanna come up here, honey?" There's a squeal of excitement from the front and we watch as a girl climbs up on to the stage.

I gasp.

It's *Isla Walsh*! How does she always seem to appear on a stage when I'm least expecting it?

We watch, our mouths hanging open, as Shani asks Isla a few questions and the next thing you know, Shani hands Isla a microphone and they actually sing "Love My Life" *together*.

"You can sing *so much* better than her." Aimee sighs in frustration. "You should be on that stage, Erin."

"So I could freeze up again?" I give her a gentle nudge. "No thanks."

At the end of the concert, we wait for the place to empty a bit before we leave our seats so we can avoid the crowds walking towards the exit.

"I really think you should have a go at auditioning," Aimee continues as we wait outside the toilets for my family. "You love Fusion. You love singing. You love dancing. And we could have so much fun making an audition video together."

"Aimee, there's no way I'd get a part. And anyway, I don't look anything like them."

"Well, you definitely *won't* get a part if you don't even try." Aimee shakes her head. "And they said they were looking for someone with a spark in their eye who could sing and dance. They didn't say you have to *look* like them."

"*Erin?*" I turn towards the voice calling my name and

try not to groan as I see Isla Walsh walking towards me from across the foyer. "I had no idea *you* were here." She pulls her long blonde ponytail over her shoulder, then throws her eyes wide. "Oh wait, you didn't see me *singing* onstage, did you? Oh, how embarrassing!" She titters, then smiles smugly as if she's not embarrassed *at all*.

"You sounded really great, Isla." I plaster a smile on my face and try to look enthusiastic.

"I'd never have thought of going onstage." Isla leans in towards me. "But, well, you heard them." She puts her hand on my arm. "They were practically *begging* me to join them."

"I think *begging* is a bit of an exaggeration," Aimee mutters from behind me as Isla glances her way. "Actually," Aimee says, pulling her shoulders back, "I was just telling Erin that *she* should audition to become a member of Fusion Junior."

"Oh." Isla's eyes grow wide. "Oh ... well, yes, of course." She wrinkles her nose. "You used to be ... *quite good* at singing, right? You should definitely *try*."

"I'm really not planning to." I shake my head.

"Hello!" The posh lady from the toilets joins us.

"Oh, Mum." Isla turns towards her. "This is Erin and Aimee. They're from my old school. They were just

14

congratulating me on my performance."

"Actually, we've already met," Isla's mum explains. "Your poor little friend Erin got stuck in the toilet. Are you OK now, sweetie?"

"Oops!" Isla giggles. "What a good job you got out. Or you might have missed my big moment."

"Oh yes." Aimee nods super seriously. "We *really* wouldn't have wanted to miss *that*."

"So does that mean that you girls will all be starting at All Saints All Girls Grammar next week?" Isla's mum changes the subject. "I hope you're not too nervous?" She gives me this really sympathetic rub on the shoulder. "Don't worry. I'm sure you'll make plenty of friends."

"Errr . . . thanks?" I say. I haven't been feeling all that nervous about starting seniors. Aimee will be with me. So, there's nothing to be too nervous about, right?

"Ready, girls?" Dad joins us and I see Mum, Nanny and Joe watching warily to one side as Mum gives her pregnant belly a tired rub. Isla's mum looks from Dad to Mum to Nanny to Joe, then back to me, a slightly puzzled expression on her face, as if she's waiting politely for us to explain something to her.

This is something that happens a *lot*.

I'm the only person in my family who has brown skin,

and people seem to find that a bit confusing, even though it's pretty simple, really.

Mum met Dad *after* I'd been born.

Up until then, Mum and I lived with Nanny.

When Dad decided that he wanted to marry Mum, he actually got down on one knee to ask *me* first, which was proper *class*. Just like Dad, really. Nanny always said that he should have got down on one knee to her too, but anyway, you'll be pleased to know that I said yes!

Luckily, so did Mum.

(And Nanny says she would have done, if Dad had bothered to ask her.)

It gets a bit boring explaining it to people and we're used to the slightly puzzled look, so we tend to just ignore it. Sometimes that can get awkward, because the person just stands there and waits for an explanation, which is what happens with Isla's mum now.

But awkward *really* doesn't bother my dad. He just smiles back really blankly as if he hasn't noticed until Isla's mum gets the hint. And then he says it's time for us to go.

"Bye, Erin." Isla waves as we walk away. "See you next week at school."

CHAPTER 3

Aimee spends the last week of the school holidays trying to convince me to audition for Fusion Junior. It's really nice that she's so convinced I could do it, so I just smile and nod every time she starts on about it, but there's *no way* I'm auditioning. Apparently, Fusion are going to be posting the competition details on their social media channels on Monday, which also happens to be my first day of senior school and Joe's first *ever* day at primary school. So, while Aimee spends the week trying to talk me into auditioning, Mum and Nanny spend the week organizing Joe and me for school.

It starts with the uniform.

School uniforms don't exactly come in our size. Actually, most clothes don't come in our size. Our arms and legs might be shorter than those of most people's our age, but our torsos are generally the same height. So we tend to buy clothes for kids our age and then Nanny shortens the arms and legs to fit. There's so much to alter with school uniforms that we spend the whole day with Nanny so that she can do it all at once.

Surprisingly enough, Joe and I *love* alteration days with Nanny.

Not the actual measuring or trying on clothes bit, because that gets properly boring. But Nanny always completely covers her dark wood dining table with plates of flapjacks and chocolate cupcakes and ginger biscuits and the whole house smells of baking, and we get to spend the day listening to the radio, playing games and watching old movies, and it's all just *really* lovely.

Aimee always comes along for alteration days too. She loves Nanny's cooking as much as Joe and I do, but she also *loves* watching Nanny sew. Last year she asked Nanny to show her how to do it, and it turns out that Aimee is *really* good at sewing. Ever since then, she doesn't just watch Nanny alter our clothes, she gets properly involved.

She's even decided that she wants to be a fashion designer when she's older. She's got these big plans to go to the London College of Fashion and create a whole range of clothes for people who have achondroplasia, because she knows how tricky it can be to buy clothes when you have dwarfism.

When Aimee told her mum and dad her plans, they said that when she's old enough to go to college, she'd be better off learning something with a better chance of success.

Something boring, like business studies.

I know, *rude*.

So, Aimee decided to actually save up her *own* money to go to fashion college.

Can you believe it?

I mean, she's eleven and she's already saving for college?

She started out by walking her neighbour's dog, Rocket, every day, and then someone up the road asked her to walk their dog too, and now she walks about five different dogs; she has a whole dog-walking business!

I think even her parents must be pretty impressed.

Anyway, I'm standing in the middle of Nanny's pink lounge carpet wearing a blazer for the third time this morning as Nanny kneels in front of me with a tape measure and two pins held between her lips. According to Nanny, the single biggest problem (so far) with starting at All Saints All Girls Seniors is *the blazer*. She's had to order six different sizes, just so that we can figure out which one can be most easily adjusted to fit me.

She takes the pins out of her mouth, rolls up the sleeves and fastens them in position, then shuffles back to look at me again.

"This is definitely the best one. Don't you think, Aimee?" She turns me by the shoulders towards her flowery sofa, where Aimee is sitting, carefully shortening a pair of Joe's trousers.

"Yep, that's the one." Aimee cuts the thread on Joe's trousers and drapes them on the arm of Nanny's sofa, along with all of the other finished bits of uniform. Nanny carefully pulls the blazer off me, takes out a pair of scissors and snips big sections of the arms off where she's folded them over. "Can I keep these?" Aimee picks up the discarded blazer arms from the floor as Nanny nods. Aimee's always keeping bits of old fabric to turn into something, or raiding Nanny's buttons and beads box. Sometimes she even drops in on Nanny to show her something that she's found in a charity shop that she plans to upcycle.

It's properly *cool*.

"Erin?" Joe clambers up on to the sofa next to Aimee, picks up the trousers and gives them a glare, as though he really doesn't like them very much, then sighs and turns towards me, his bottom lip looking a bit wobbly. "Will I really like school?"

This is a question that Joe has been asking me a *lot* recently and it's a tricky one. Joe *hates* the attention that comes with having dwarfism. He's only five and he hides behind my legs every time we go out anywhere new.

Starting school is *major* to Joe.

He already knows that he'll get noticed by the other kids, and he already knows that he'll be told that he's small and called cute or, if he's unlucky, something worse.

He also knows that he won't have my legs to hide behind.

"I really hope so, Joe," I reply, because I never lie to Joe when it comes to people's reactions to our achondroplasia. And knowing how Joe feels about attention, I can't promise that he's going to love school right away. "I met Aimee on the first day of primary school." I touch his arm. "Maybe you'll make an amazing best friend on your first day too."

Joe nods slowly as he looks at the floor and tugs at his sleeve. He does *not* look convinced.

"And you've got that nice Miss King as your teacher." Nanny passes him a chocolate fairy cake from the table.

"Erin really liked her, didn't you, Erin?"

"Oh, yeah, she was *so* nice," I agree. "*And* you've got Liam as your class helper. He's the best!" Liam was my class helper until the end of last year, and I know that Joe will love him. He's so much fun, and he never made me feel any different. He was there if I needed him, but he could also fade into the background. I'm really glad that Joe's going to have him now.

Just for a second, I wonder what my new class helper will be like at seniors next week. I hope they're like Liam.

I smile brightly as Joe gives me that resigned look that he sometimes has when he knows he has to do something but he'd really rather not, so I pull out my trump card. "You remember about Liam's black belt in kung fu?" Joe wants to be a kung fu master when he's older. "And he runs the after-school kung fu club. You're bound to get a place with Liam as your helper."

Joes shrugs and looks at the floor. Still not convinced.

"Hey, Joe." Aimee shuffles up the sofa towards him. "Can you show me your best kung fu kick?"

Joe shrugs again and shakes his head. He's not going to be distracted *that* easily.

"Have you forgotten, Joe?" I climb up on to the sofa next to him. "You can do *anything*."

Joe sighs, gets down from the sofa, gets into the classic kung fu position and does a totally profesh kung fu kick.

"With moves like that you'll be a black belt in no time!" Aimee laughs and Joe's face lights up, his worries about school parked for now as he does another kung fu kick with this really menacing face. I meet Aimee's eyes and give her a grateful smile just as "Love My Life" starts to play on Nanny's old radio. Aimee goes over to turn it up and Joe carries on practising his kung fu moves as we all wiggle our shoulders and sing along, even Nanny.

"Don't *you* think that Erin should audition for Fusion Junior?" Aimee asks Nanny as the song finishes, then gives me this really knowing wiggle of her eyebrows.

"Aimee!" I give her a playful smack on the arm as I laugh. "How many times? I'm not applying. I can't sing in front of people, remember? And anyway, there's *no way* I'd get selected." I hesitate. Joe's watching me really carefully as he tucks into his chocolate fairy cake.

"Why not?" Nanny asks. "You've got a lovely singing voice."

"Exactly." Aimee nods firmly.

"And have you forgotten, Erin?" Joe copies my words as he speaks through a mouthful of chocolate cake, a massive cheeky grin on his face: "You can do *anything*."

I laugh and give Joe's hair a fond ruffle as I think back to when I was on stage.

That moment that I took a breath for the second time, ready to try again.

I often wonder if I could have actually done it. If I would have started singing if Isla hadn't taken things into her own hands.

But the truth is I don't really know. And knowing how bad I felt after choking onstage, I'm not ready to find out.

CHAPTER 4

I hit snooze on the alarm. I cannot believe that it's my first day of secondary school today. I've been so busy trying to reassure Joe about *his* first day that I haven't really thought about mine.

I turn towards my uniform hanging up on my bedroom mirror, next to all of my Fusion posters and Polaroid photos washi-taped to the wall, and take a deep breath. Nanny has done an amazing job on my blazer, but Aimee's made an adjustment to it as well and it makes it *even better*: on the inside pocket (where nobody other than me can see it) she's sewn this little image that looks a bit like a sideways figure of eight but is actually a *friends for ever* symbol. She's got one on the inside of her blazer too, so that if we find ourselves separated at school, then we can just look at our inside pockets and it will cheer us right up.

I *love it*.

I really hope we don't get separated, though, because that would be a proper disaster. But before I have a chance to think too much about that, my alarm goes off again.

I sit up and rub my eyes.

"Erin?" Joe's standing in the doorway of my bedroom, his mousy hair ruffled, his *PAW Patrol* pyjamas crumpled, his bottom lip turned down. "I don't feel well. I don't think I can go to school today."

"Aw, Joe." I get down from my bed and give him a hug. "It's going to be OK. Liam will make sure that everything goes well." Joe snuggles in, then stands back and looks me right in the eyes.

"Do you *promise*, Erin?"

Joe takes promises *super* seriously and believe me, I found that out the hard way. Last year, I made Joe this wild promise that I'd take him to Disneyland if he'd let me have the last Jaffa cake in the biscuit tin. He trusted me so much that he actually went upstairs and packed. When Mum told him that I couldn't keep my promise, he didn't believe her at first. In the end, I had to tell him and he was so upset. He didn't speak for *two whole weeks* after that and I felt properly awful about it. I never want to feel like that again.

So, if I make a promise to Joe, I really have to *mean* it.

I might not be able to make any promises about how his day will go, but I can definitely promise that Liam is really ace.

I smile and say confidently, "I *promise* that Liam will be a great class helper for you, and he will make your day as good as it can be."

Joe meets my eyes as if checking whether he can really believe me, then finally he nods and walks back to his room.

"Erin!" Mum marches up the stairs. "Your taxi will be here in an hour. You need to get ready."

An hour later and I'm standing in the doorway of our house watching the drizzle outside as I wait for my taxi to arrive to take me to school.

All Saints All Girls Seniors is the opposite end of town from St Winifred's, which is Joe's primary school, so from now on Mum will be taking Joe to school in the car and I'm getting a taxi.

When Mum first told me that I wouldn't be getting the school bus with Aimee, because the steps are too high for my legs and I could easily get knocked over if it was busy, I wasn't dead pleased. But now that I'm standing here watching some other kids run to the bus stop in the pouring rain, I can't help thinking that maybe a taxi isn't so bad after all. It must get super annoying to have to wait for a bus every day.

My taxi arrives dead on time. It's a minivan taxi and it's driven by a nice, slightly bald man called Pat. He gets out of the car and opens the door for me and tells me not to worry because he's a very careful driver. Then he looks at his watch and tells me that we'll arrive at school at exactly 8.48 a.m.

"Errrr. OK." I shrug as I climb into the taxi. That was a bit precise.

"So, how was your morning so far today, Erin?" Pat asks as he pulls away from my house *super* slowly.

"It was great, thank you." I smile politely and look out of the window as a bike zips past us. When Pat said that he was a careful driver, I guess what he really meant was *slow*.

"Oh, that's grand. Mine was great too," Pat replies. "I woke up this morning to find out that I won the lottery last night. This taxi driver's a multi-millionaire!"

"What? Really?" I lean forwards, then meet Pat's eyes

in the rear-view mirror as he chuckles and winks. Oh. I sit back. A classic dad joke. Except . . . two can play at that game.

"Actually. . ." I sit forward, a sparkle in my eyes. "Something amazing happened to me this morning too." I try to think of something that would be completely amazing, something that would be as good as winning the lottery.

"What would that be then, Erin?" Pat asks as I wrack my brains. There's got to be *something*, so I say the first thing that pops into my head.

"I woke up to find out that I've been made the newest member of Fusion Junior." I laugh, then stop, my smile dropping just a little as I imagine myself standing onstage with Fusion. That would be even *better* than winning the lottery. I shake my head. But that's never going to happen.

"Well, I'd better drive even more carefully then, hadn't I?" Pat plays along. "Didn't realize I had a pop star in the back of my taxi."

"I don't think you *could* drive all that much more carefully, Pat." I give Pat a cheeky grin as the school bus overtakes us.

We arrive at school at precisely 8.48 a.m.

"Told you." Pat opens my door, his shoulders held back proudly.

"Thanks, Pat." I let my feet drop from the taxi to the ground, turn towards the school gates and take a deep breath.

"Aw, look!" I turn back as an older girl in uniform nudges her friend and points at me. "Is it just me, or are the new intakes getting *smaller*? She is *so cute*."

"Erin!" Aimee runs towards me. "I was too scared to walk in without you. This place is properly *huge*." She glances over her shoulder at the school and sidles towards me.

"Don't worry." I open my blazer to show her the friendship symbol on my inside pocket as Aimee takes a deep breath and nods uncertainly. "We'll be OK." I try to look way more confident than I'm feeling and we start walking in through the big iron gates together.

"Isla was on the bus this morning." Aimee pulls her bag over her shoulder nervously as we try not to notice that a few of the other girls have looked up to watch as we walk past and focus on the signs directing us towards the hall. "She was telling everyone about her *big* moment onstage with Fusion. The way she's talking about it, you'd think she's their new best friend!" We stop walking as this big blowsy lady blocks the path in front of us, her hand to her heart, her eyes all wide as she stares really hard at *me*.

"Errrr. Who's that?" I lean in and whisper to Aimee.

"I'm not sure." Aimee mutters. "Do you think she's OK? Why is she *staring* at you like that?" I check over one shoulder, then the other. I'm used to getting strange reactions from people, but this is even stranger than usual. "Is she . . . having a heart attack?" Aimee hisses. But before I have a chance to answer, the woman walks towards me really slowly and hesitantly, as if she might scare me with any sudden movements.

"Errrr. Hi?" I give the lady a tight smile. The kind that says, *I want to be nice, but you're creeping me out a bit.*

"Erin?" she says, her face all flushed like this is the most *exciting* moment of her *whole life*.

"Yeah?" My *I'm nice; you're creepy* smile remains firmly in place.

Who is this woman?

"It's *me*." She gets down on to her knees and spreads her arms out. She's not seriously expecting me to hug her, is she?

Never gonna happen, lady.

"I'm Barbara . . . your new class helper."

Oh. No.

"Ahhhhh." I try so hard to look pleased to meet her, when all I really want to do right now is to run for the hills.

"I know I'm not supposed to call you *cute*," she gushes, "but you really are just *adorable*."

Aimee's jaw drops open.

"Well, let's get going, shall we?" Barbara lumbers off her knees, before giving Aimee a curt nod to let her know that she'll be taking it from here. "Say goodbye to your little friend."

There's a giggle from ahead and I see Isla Walsh watching as she has a whispered conversation behind her hand with her best friend, Sophia.

I literally want the ground to swallow me up right now. I've always had a class helper and it's never been a problem. But my class helpers normally stay in the *background*. They never make a big fuss over me. Because, well … they understand that it's majorly *embarrassing*. Like now. I just need someone to carry my bag for me and maybe open the odd door, if the handle's too high, or reach for something I need. But their role is definitely *never* to single me out or take me away from my best friend, and anyway, I didn't think I was supposed to meet my class helper until I got to my new form room.

"I think I'm supposed to go to the hall first thing." I try to back away. "We're supposed to be meeting *after* registration, right?"

"You don't need to go to the hall." Barbara tugs my bag off my shoulder. "I've already picked up your timetable. I'll take you straight to your form room."

"Oh." I hesitate, my eyes darting towards Aimee. "Is Aimee in the same form as me?"

"Aimee?" Barbara seems to have forgotten that she's still here. "I wouldn't know, dear." She shakes her head. "Come on," she orders as she starts marching towards a big red double doorway at the end of the school driveway.

"Do I *have* to go with her?" I whisper to Aimee.

"I guess?" Aimee sighs. She looks as hesitant as I feel. "She seems to be really excited about working with you. Maybe give her a chance, yeah? And don't worry." She nods really firmly. "They'll *definitely* keep us together." I can't help wondering which of us she's trying to convince as she rubs her thumb along the friendship symbol on her inside pocket distractedly.

I smile as I put my hand on her arm. "We're going to have a brilliant first day of school, Aimee." I try to ignore Barbara waiting on the path just ahead of us, hopping from one foot to the other. "I just know it."

CHAPTER 5

We do *not* have a brilliant first day of school.

It starts with Barbara leading me down this really huge white corridor covered in noticeboards as she carries my bag, talking non-stop about how special it is to be my helper and how she'll make sure that I'm treated the same as all the other girls, even though the person who has treated me the most differently since I arrived here so far is *Barbara*.

We walk along the tiled hallway to an old lift where she pulls out this credit card type thing and tells me it's the lift key. Apparently, she'll let me have one at the end of the day once she's shown me how to use it properly. Then she tells me how my form class is on the second floor and how she'll meet me at the gates *every* day to carry my bag and take me to class.

"Oh." I try not to sigh. *"Great."*

When we reach the second floor, Barbara leads me down another white, tiled corridor and into my form room, where a tall, slim lady with the most amazing braids is writing on the whiteboard.

Welcome to All Saints!

She seems quite young to be a teacher. She's wearing a crisp shirt and a pencil skirt with sensible heels, and she looks quite serious. Most of my old teachers were smiley and way less sensibly dressed. But then I notice that her shirt has tiny pink llamas printed all over it. Maybe she's not as serious as she seems.

She turns towards us with this really puzzled expression as Barbara puts her hands on my shoulders and says, "Miss Wilson. *This* is Erin." And then she whispers really theatrically, "Isn't she *adorable?*"

I hear Miss Wilson's slight intake of breath and for a second, she says *literally nothing*.

Her eyes flick from Barbara to me until finally she smiles and says, "Welcome to the class, Erin." Then she looks up at Barbara, her smile remaining in place but her eyes hardening, just a little. "Shouldn't this student be in the *hall* with everyone else?"

"Oh." Barbara's face falls. "Well, I just thought that it would be nice to give Erin a chance to see her classroom before anyone else arrived."

"I can see that was well-intentioned" – Miss Wilson straightens a pile of paperwork on her desk, before meeting Barbara's gaze with a firm but polite nod – "but I don't think it was necessary. I'm sure Erin would much rather have remained with her *friends*."

I try really hard not to gasp as my mouth drops open and I snap it shut again before Barbara or Miss Wilson notice.

"Oh." Barbara takes her hands off my shoulders as I pretend to be amazingly interested in some artwork on the wall, even though I'm secretly thinking that Miss Wilson is properly *class*. "Oh. Of course," she replies. "I'm sorry, I didn't think."

"Please don't worry." Miss Wilson picks up a clipboard from her desk. "We'll just put it down to first-day nerves." She turns back to me. "Erin, I'm going to collect the rest of the form from the hall now. Would you like to join me, or are you happy to stay here?"

I kind of want to join her.

But then I look at Barbara. She looks pretty mortified.

She's gone a bit red and starts tucking in chairs and trying to look busy and I can't help feeling a bit sorry for her, so I tell Miss Wilson that I'll wait here.

"OK," Miss Wilson agrees. "If you'd like to choose a desk, I'll be back in five minutes."

"Miss Wilson?" I ask as she reaches the door. "Is Aimee Dowling in this form?"

She glances down at her clipboard for Aimee's name, then looks back up, the corners of her mouth creeping up. "She is, Erin." She tucks the clipboard under her arm, then sweeps out of the room and I grin so wide, because maybe my first day of school will get better after all.

It doesn't.

In fact, being in a form with Aimee and getting to sit next to her in form time is probably the *only* thing that goes right.

First of all, Aimee isn't the only person I know from primary school.

Isla Walsh and her best friend, Sophia, are in our form too.

Isla struts into the room behind Miss Wilson as the class are led in, then stops as she sees me. "Oh, Erin! How lovely to see you!" She looks from me to Barbara, this fixed smile on her face as Barbara bends down to straighten the stool next to my chair. "And what an *attentive* class helper you have." She shares a smirk with Sophia as Barbara lumbers back up.

"That's right." Barbara crosses her arms as she looks down her nose at them. "I intend to help Erin any way that she needs." She looks properly menacing and I can't help wondering if Barbara's got a bit confused and thinks that she's my bodyguard rather than my class helper. Isla looks from Barbara to me as I pretend not to notice, even though I can feel my face going red. Finally, she gives me a tight smile, then sweeps away with Sophia to find chairs at the back of the class.

Miss Wilson tells us to get into groups of four, then gives us a map of the school and says that we're going to be doing a treasure hunt to learn our way around.

Aimee and I team up with these two girls called Morgan and Grace. Morgan has bright ginger curls pulled back into a high ponytail and a face full of freckles and Grace has black skin and the most incredible space buns. It probably shouldn't surprise me that there's another black girl in my class, but for some reason it does.

The four of us start chatting and laughing and getting

to know each other and I wonder if today might actually turn out to be quite fun.

Then Barbara joins us.

She keeps interrupting us when we're looking at the map and asking really loudly if I'm *OK* or if I need any *help*.

And as if that wasn't annoying enough, she doesn't let Aimee, Morgan or Grace use the lift with me either, so I have to keep separating from them every time we come to a staircase.

When we get back to class, Barbara makes a big show of patting the cushion on my chair, and even though I know she thinks she's being nice, it's really annoying. Liam *never* used to do any of this stuff. I hope Joe's having a better day with Liam than I am with Barbara.

It's a bit of a relief when I get a break from her at lunchtime.

"Maybe she'll be less . . . *helpful* in a few days." Aimee lifts my school dinner tray down to me.

"I really hope so." I take it from her. It's spaghetti bolognese, my favourite! At least there's one thing that's going right today.

"Well, if she isn't, then you should talk to your mum about it," Aimee suggests as we look around the enormous hall, so full of tables and chairs and older children larking about, that I have no idea how we're going to find somewhere to sit.

"Yeah, I guess so," I sigh.

"Hey, Erin! Hey, Aimee!" Morgan and Grace wave at us from one of the lunch tables. "Join us?"

I meet Aimee's eyes and she nods, so we head over towards them. But just as I'm climbing on to the seat, Isla and Sophia join us too.

"Hi, girls." Isla sits down confidently right opposite me. "So, how's everyone finding their first day?" She pulls her ponytail over her shoulder as she looks around the table. "Oh, Erin." She reaches her hand towards me. "I'm so pleased that you weren't stuck in the toilet for too long at the Fusion concert last week."

"Errr . . . thanks, Isla." I smile through gritted teeth as the lunch table goes a bit quiet and awkward.

Why did she have to mention *that*?

"I've been locked in the toilets before." Morgan gives me a friendly nudge. "It was *so* embarrassing. I was—"

"Anyway," Isla interrupts with a dismissive roll of her eyes, "thank goodness your nan had that baby stool for you to use, or you might have missed the whole concert! And you know, *I* was so happy to see you there too." She puts her hand on her heart. "It's not easy performing onstage with Fusion, it really meant a lot to see a friendly face."

"Huh?" Grace's head darts towards Isla. *"You were onstage with Fusion?"*

"Oh, silly me, I've gone and mentioned it *again*." Isla flaps her hand in front of her face as if she's really embarrassed that someone knows about it, even though that's obviously why she started this whole conversation in the first place. "Actually. . ." She leans into the table. "I'm just waiting for the competition details so that I can start on my audition tape for Fusion Junior. It's going live on their social media platforms this afternoon." Aimee gives me a little kick under the table along with this really significant nod, and Isla notices. "Oh, that's right. You were thinking of auditioning, weren't you, Erin?"

"Not really." I concentrate on twirling spaghetti around my fork. "I mean. . ." I pause. "Well, it would be *so* amazing." I remember my daydream from earlier in the taxi. "But. . ." I shake my head. "I don't really like to sing in front of people."

"Oh. Yes." Isla puts her head to one side sympathetically. "I *remember*."

"Are you good at singing, then, Erin?" Morgan asks.

"She's *so* good." Aimee leans forward, but before

anyone has a chance to say anything more, Isla's phone starts ringing loudly.

Isla puts her hand up, as if she's hitting pause on our conversation. She rolls her shoulders back and smooths down her hair, like she's preparing for something really important, then scrunches up her nose and says, "Sorry, I need to get this."

We all watch as she stands up and walks literally a metre away from the lunch table to answer her phone. "OMG, no *way!*" She squeals seconds later as everyone around her stops to listen. "Fusion have sent you the details early? Oh, that's *amazing!*" She turns towards us, her hand raised to her chest, her eyes all wide and sparkly. Then she grabs her bag and sweeps out of the room, still on the phone as Sophia chases after her.

CHAPTER 6

"Told you." Pat smiles proudly as he opens the door of the taxi outside my house. "4.18 p.m. precisely."

"Nailed it, Pat." I let my feet drop wearily to the pavement from the seat of the taxi. Even with Pat's super slow driving, I'm so happy to get a taxi to school. When the bus overtook us earlier, it looked properly *rammed*.

"See you tomorrow at 8.20 a.m." Pat taps his watch as he opens the taxi door to get back in.

"Don't be late." I grin cheekily. "You don't want to keep this pop star waiting."

Pat stops and turns back to me with a chuckle. "Well, you'd better keep your eyes peeled because I might pick you up in a stretch limousine tomorrow." He winks, then gets into the old minivan and carefully pulls away.

I walk in through the back door to a quiet house.

Mum said she'd be home from collecting Joe after me and Dad had a night shift, so he'll be asleep. He works as the night manager at this really posh hotel called the Grand Central in Belfast, so he has to sleep a lot in the daytime, and we all have to tiptoe around.

I drop my bag in the hallway and head straight for the biscuit tin.

Home is the one place that I never have to think about my size. Everything's been lowered or adjusted so that it's all within reach. Light switches, kitchen counters and most importantly, biscuit tins.

I take out three Jaffa cakes.

After lunch, the rest of the day had *not* get better.

In fact, it got a *billion* times worse. Definitely a three Jaffa cake kind of day.

I put a whole Jaffa cake in my mouth, then take another one out of the biscuit tin.

Maybe even a *four* Jaffa cake kind of day.

And believe me, that means it was a really bad day. I don't put the lid back on the biscuit tin, just in case.

We spent all afternoon running over our timetables and it turns out that Aimee and I *only* have PE together.

That's literally *two* lessons! One on a Tuesday and one on a Friday. I don't have *any* other lessons with her.

Not *one*!

So, even though we're in the same form, we won't actually be together that much *at all*.

It's a total disaster.

Aimee and I have spent every day of school together since primary. We *have* to be together. We even tried telling Miss Wilson that I need to be with Aimee in all of my lessons, just in case Barbara isn't there one day and I need some help. But Miss Wilson just said that *anyone* in my class can help me if Barbara's not available and that from what she could see, I had a mouth and I should know how to ask for help if I need it.

I know, it turns out Miss Wilson isn't as class as I thought.

At least I'm in quite a lot of classes with Morgan; she seems really nice. But poor Aimee has loads of classes with Isla, so she's not happy *at all*.

I put another Jaffa cake in my mouth and look out of the window as I wait for Aimee to arrive.

Aimee's parents are both doctors and they work at weird times, so our parents have an arrangement that Aimee can come over to our house after school whenever they're working. Some weeks it means that she's here every day, which is properly brilliant, especially when she brings Rocket along too.

I don't have to wait too long.

When Aimee arrives, she walks in through the back door, marches straight to the biscuit tin and takes out three Jaffa cakes. She puts one in her mouth, meets my eyes, raises her eyebrows, then takes out another.

You see? A four Jaffa cake kind of day.

"Do you think your mum could *make* the school keep us together?" she asks through a mouthful of Jaffa cake.

"Maybe?" I shrug. "I could ask her?"

Aimee's phone pings as we both munch on our biscuits and she takes it out of her pocket to look at it.

"Oh, Erin!" She suddenly looks really excited.

"What's happened?" I ask as Rocket starts running around in circles by the back door. I guess he's picked up on all the excited energy that Aimee's giving out.

"It's the competition details for Fusion Junior! They've posted it!" Aimee squeals as Rocket starts barking really excitedly by her legs. Aimee opens the back door and Rocket bolts into the garden and does a wee in Dad's favourite rose bush. I guess it wasn't excitement after all. "Do you want to have a look at it?" Aimee nudges me.

I've got to admit, I'm kind of *intrigued* to see it, even

if I'm not planning to audition.

"You might even feel like making an audition video after you've seen it." Aimee sidles up to me as Rocket runs back in through the back door and pants by my feet, his tail thumping the floor. "See! Even Rocket wants you to look at it." Aimee giggles.

"Why do you want me to audition so much, anyway?" I can't help asking as I laugh.

"Because you're such a great singer!" Aimee exclaims. "And this is what you always wanted. I know it's a bit of a long shot, but what's the harm in *trying*?" She gives me a little nudge. "Who cares if you're not what they're looking for. You're amazing, and you should show them that anyway. Imagine! Fusion watching your video. Please, Erin, I've been thinking we could have loads of fun with it. Like we used to when we were younger. We always had so much fun making up plays and stuff. You could make me your creative director. I've already had some ideas. I think I could make it *so* good! At least look at Fusion's video about it." She lifts up her phone and raises her eyebrows as Shani, Brooke and Robin from Fusion smile out at us from the screen.

"All right then." I nod as her eyes light up and she presses play.

"Heeeey, Belfast!" They all wave at the camera. "You

may have heard that we're asking kids to audition for Fusion Junior. Well, here are the deets!"

Shani leans forward and talks directly into the camera. "Our new song is about friendship, and we're looking for three future stars to create a Fusion Junior group to feature in the music video, which we'll be making in. . ."

"Belfast!" they all say together.

"To be invited to audition, your dancing talent and star quality must really shine through." Brooke's talking now. "All you need to do is to make a five-minute audition video and email it to our team."

"But!" Robin's turn to talk. "Places are limited. So make sure you send us the best video you can. We want to see girls who can really sing and dance."

"At the end of this video –" Shani leans forward again, her face a bit more serious now – "follow the link to hear our newest song, 'Together'."

"*Learn it, guys!*" Robin points at the camera.

"Then send us a video of *you* singing it. Followed by a two-minute clip to show us your dance moves!" Brooke shimmies at the camera. "You can dance to anything you like, so make sure you send us something that really shows us who you are!"

"Good luck, everybody!" The whole group wave at the

camera again. "Hopefully we'll meet you soon!"

Aimee clicks on the link and we listen to their new song, "Together".

It's *really* good and so catchy, especially the chorus.

"Wow." I sit back after we've listened to it three more times. "That song is going to be major."

"And you'd sound so amazing singing it." Aimee raises her eyebrows. "Please, Erin. Can we make an audition video together, *pleeeeeaaaase?*"

I meet Aimee's eyes, my mouth twitching at the corners. I guess it would be fun to make a video together. And well, I know it's really unlikely but ... what if I actually got into Fusion Junior? That would be pretty amazing, wouldn't it?

"Fine." I roll my eyes, but I can't hold in my grin for one second longer. "Let's do it."

CHAPTER 7

"So, if we're really doing this..." Aimee puts her bag down on my bedroom floor five minutes later and walks towards my white desk decisively as I follow behind, the biscuit tin cradled in my hands. "... we'd better make a plan." She takes a piece of scrap paper out of my drawer and starts making a list.

FUSION JUNIOR AUDITION TO-DO LIST

1. Learn "Together".
2. Record Erin singing "Together".
3. Choose music for dance video.
4. Record dance video.
5. Edit audition video.
6. Send audition video to Fusion.

"Easy, right?" She looks up from her list, her eyes bright. Aimee *loves* making lists. She pauses as she notices the biscuit tin in my hand, then adds:

7. Get more Jaffa cakes.

"Aims?" I ask nervously. "What about the whole freezing when I sing in public thing? What if I actually got an audition? I don't want to choke again, especially not in front of Fusion!"

"Well, don't worry about that too much just yet; let's focus on the video first." Aimee chews my pen thoughtfully. "But maybe we should get you some practice at singing in public?" She adds 8. Practise singing in public to the list.

"And we'll probably need to come up with some kind of a dance routine," I carry on as Aimee adds that to the list too. "And I guess we should think about what I'd wear."

"Oooh, well, I've already got an idea for the outfit." Aimee picks up my denim jacket from the bed. "Can I keep hold of this?"

"Of course!" as I point down to Aimee's phone. "They didn't mention a deadline. Is there more info somewhere on their website?"

Aimee flicks on to their website and we take a look. There's actually quite a bit of extra information, starting with a three-week deadline.

"Do you think that gives us enough time?" I ask.

"Yeah. Definitely." Aimee nods. "But you'll need to start learning 'Together' right away so we can record you singing it this weekend."

We scroll on. In small print right at the bottom, it says:

PLEASE NOTE:
You must have parental permission to send a video.
Parents/guardians will be required to attend
if you are invited to audition.

Aimee meets my eyes.

"Your mum and dad will be OK with this, right?" she asks.

I hesitate because I haven't really thought about that.

Dad can be pretty relaxed about most things, but Mum might take a *little* bit of persuading. I can already imagine her talking about how I need to concentrate on my schoolwork and avoid getting too tired.

"I *think* so. But it might be best if we don't mention about Barbara . . . or not being in many classes together in school . . . or anything much that's happened today."

"OK." Aimee bites her lip. "But will that *really* make

a difference? I was hoping your mum would make the school keep us together."

"I'm not sure." I frown. "Maybe? I just don't want to give Mum a reason to say no. So, let's keep things light and breezy. If anyone asks, we can just say that we're in a form together and that we had spaghetti bolognese for school dinners."

"Erin? Aimee?" Mum hollers up the stairs. "We're going to McDonald's to celebrate the first day of school. You ready?"

"Just a minute!" I call down as Aimee pulls out a hoodie and a pair of jeans from her school bag, and we quickly change out of our school uniforms.

"You could ask them while we're at McDonald's?" Aimee tugs her hoodie over her head.

"I think it might work best to ask when Nanny's there too." I give myself a quick check in the mirror, pull my school headband off and tease my Afro out so it's a bit bigger.

"Oh, good idea." Aimee agrees. "She seemed keen when I mentioned it last week at her house. She'll definitely support you."

"Come on, girls! Aimee still needs to take Rocket home, and we've said we'll pick up Nanny on the way."

Aimee and I meet each other's eyes, our faces lighting up.

"That's perfect!" Aimee picks up Rocket's lead from the bed. "I'll take Rocket home now and then you can ask your mum and dad at McDonald's." She opens the door. "See you in a minute." She gives me an enthusiastic thumbs up, then runs down the stairs.

"What do you mean that Joe doesn't want to do kung fu any more?" I overhear Dad talking to Mum in the kitchen as I come down a few minutes later.

"I'm not sure." Mum looks up as I walk in. "He just said he doesn't want to do kung fu any more. I asked his class helper about it, but she didn't seem to know anything about it."

"*She?*" I ask. "What about Liam?"

"Apparently, Liam's been asked to work with a different child," Mum explains. "Joe has a helper called Sarah. She seems lovely."

"But I *promised* Joe that he'd have Liam." My voice sounds all breathless and worried. All I can think about is what if Joe reacts like the last time I broke a promise? What if he doesn't talk for two weeks again? "I told him that Liam would take him to the school kung fu club."

"Oh, Erin." Mum's face fills with understanding. "You

know how seriously he takes promises." The image of Joe's crushed little face when I told him that he wouldn't be going to Disneyland pops into my head. "You'd better go straight up and talk to him." Mum glances nervously at the stairs. "We're still waiting for Aimee to get back from dropping off Rocket. You should go up there now. And let's hope he gets over this one a bit quicker than last time." She sighs.

I grab the biscuit tin and clamber up the stairs.

"Hey, Joe." I walk into Joe's room, the biscuit tin held in front of me as a peace offering. He's lying on his PAW-Patrol-duvet-covered bed, facing the wall. This does not look good. I shut the door carefully behind me. "Everything OK?" I climb on to the edge of his bed, hoping that it's a good sign that he shuffles along to make room for me. "So, how was your first day of school?" I keep my voice breezy, as if I don't know anything.

Joe doesn't answer right away. He just keeps staring at the wall while I fidget, feeling awkward as I wait for him to reply.

"You lied." He finally rounds on me, his bottom lip trembling, and even though he's angry, I'm just relieved that he's talking. "I don't have Liam as my class helper. I've got Sarah. You broke your promise." He doesn't say *again*, but we both know he's thinking it.

"I'm so sorry, Joe." I put my hand on his arm. I don't ever want Joe to think that he can't trust me. "I didn't know that you weren't going to have Liam. You know I'd never make you a promise if I didn't believe it. Not after last time." I open the biscuit tin and hold it out towards him. "Don't you like Sarah, then?" I try and keep him talking.

"She's OK." Joe shrugs as he sits up and takes a Jaffa cake out of the tin. "But now I can't do kung fu."

"What? Why not?" I sit up really straight, my whole face one big question mark. "You can still do kung fu whether Liam's your helper or not."

"Alfie says that I can't do kung fu." Joe takes a tiny nibble of Jaffa cake, a big fat tear rolling down his cheek. "He says that I'm too short." He swipes the tear from his face.

"*Who's Alfie?*" My fists clench. "Is he a boy in your class?" Joe nods and takes another forlorn nibble of Jaffa cake. "Well, Alfie doesn't know what he's talking about." I help myself to another Jaffa cake. Maybe it's a five Jaffa cake day. "You can do whatever you want, Joe. Being small doesn't have to stop us from doing *anything*."

Joe doesn't look convinced. He looks me right in the

eye as if he's trying to decide if I'm telling the truth, then he sighs and says, "You don't really think that."

"Of course I do," I retort.

"No, you don't." Joe shakes his head really certainly. "I heard you at Nanny's. You said that you can't audition to be in Fusion Junior, even if you are good at singing, because they'd never pick you. *You* don't think you can do anything, and I *can't* do kung fu." He glares at me.

"Well, actually. . ." I smile. "I *am* going to audition to be in Fusion Junior. So you see, I *do* believe that we can do anything." I stuff the entire Jaffa cake in my mouth.

"Really?" Joe turns towards me, his eye wide.

"Mm-hmm." I nod, my mouth full of biscuit.

"Do you promise?" Joe asks.

"Of course I promise!" I say through my mouthful. "I said that I'm trying, didn't I? You can ask Aimee." I wave my hand dismissively towards the door. "We've already started making a plan."

"No." Joe shakes his head. "Do you promise that you'll get *into* Fusion Junior? That we can be *anything*. Like you said."

I stop chewing.

"Look, Joe, I'll definitely try. . ." I gulp down the last of my biscuit. How can I possibly *promise* that I'll get into

Fusion Junior? I'm not even sure if I'll be able to sing in front of them, let alone get selected to join them. But then I turn back to Joe as he waits for me to tell him if I really believe that he can do *anything* and . . . how can I *not* promise?

"I. . ." I'm not sure if it's all the Jaffa cakes, but my mouth feels so dry. "I. . ." I cough, then meet Joe's burning gaze, my shoulders dropping in defeat. "All right then, Joe." I sigh. "I *promise*."

CHAPTER 8

I try really hard not to think about the promise I just made to Joe as we all squeeze into our seven-seater, ready to head to McDonald's. The car's been adjusted for Mum to drive, so Dad climbs sleepily into the back with us, leaving the passenger seat free for Nanny.

"Everything OK?" Aimee smiles as she squeezes in next to me.

"Yeah, course." I nod as I try to ignore the funny feeling in my belly.

Aimee knows all about the whole Disneyland Jaffa cake saga. In fact, she wasn't dead impressed with me when I made that promise to Joe. I can already picture her face if I tell her about this. Not to mention that she'll probably badger me to tell Joe that I can't keep my promise and I *really* don't want to do that.

So, I guess I just have to make sure I get a part in Fusion Junior.

My stomach clenches.

"Look at this, Erin!" Joe bounces into the seat next to me and karate chops the air.

"Whoa! That's amazing, Joe." I'm so glad that I've made Joe feel better and I try to look enthusiastic, even though my chest is feeling a bit tight. Joe demonstrates a straight punch into the driver's seat headrest.

"Hey!" Mum calls from the driver's seat as her head jerks forwards. "No kung fu in the car, please, Joe."

"Feeling better now, Buddy?" Dad yawns as he ruffles Joe's hair. Joe nods *really* enthusiastically and Dad gives me a grateful smile.

"How was your first day at All Saints, girls?" Nanny asks as she gets into the car.

Aimee meets my eye and I try to forget about the whole promise thing as I bob my head to let her know that I've got this. Keeping things light and breezy. Sticking to the plan.

"It went..." I pause as I look at Joe sitting quietly on the seat next to me. I really hope that he'll be OK at school tomorrow. "... *all right*," I finish slightly unenthusiastically.

"*All right?*" Nanny and Mum repeat in perfect unison, and I kick myself. Mum and Nanny can sniff out an unspoken problem quicker than a shark can sniff out blood. Why didn't I just say "good" with a big, bright smile?

"Well, yeah. It was *fine*," I try again, and Aimee elbows me, because I think even she can see that I'm doing the world's worst job of keeping things light and breezy.

"*Fine?*" they both repeat again, and Nanny's head swivels round towards me like an owl, her eyes sharp. I plaster a beaming smile on my face and try for the third time.

"It was really good." I say as brightly as I can.

"Well, even I'm worried now." Dad looks up from his phone.

"Yes, Erin, that doesn't sound good at all." Nanny watches me closely. "What happened?"

"Nothing." I shake my head. Nanny doesn't blink. "Really, nothing happened."

Nanny turns towards Aimee.

"What happened, Aimee?" she asks.

"Errr..." Aimee's eyes grow wide, and I can almost see the cogs whirring as she tries to decide how she's supposed to answer. "Well ... we ... had spaghetti bolognese for school dinners?"

"*Spaghetti bolognese?*" Mum and Nanny both repeat as I shoot Aimee a look. Spaghetti bolognese was supposed to be a *good* thing.

"Was it not a nice spaghetti bolognese, then?" Nanny peers at Aimee. "Too much onion?" She raises her eyebrows knowingly. "It's an easy mistake to make."

"Errr . . . yes?" Aimee throws her eyes really wide. "So much onion." She gives me a sage nod to let me know that she's got the situation handled. "And. . ." She leans forward really seriously. "*No garlic bread.*"

"Tsk, no garlic bread!" Nanny exclaims as everyone in the car shakes their heads at the very thought of a spaghetti bolognese with no garlic bread. "I thought All Saints was supposed to be a *good* school." Nanny turns towards Mum accusingly as Aimee gives me a little thumbs up.

"And that was it?" Mum peers at me in the rear-view mirror. "A spaghetti bolognese with too much onion and no garlic bread made your day *all right?*"

"Well, yeah?" I reply a little unconvincingly.

"I don't think so, Erin Woods." Mum shakes her head. "Spill it."

I consider telling her that there was no custard with our apple pie, but then I meet Mum's eye. I can't get *anything* past her.

"It's no big deal." I sigh. "It's only that my class helper was a bit annoying."

"Oh." Mum's shoulders drop.

Clearly an annoying helper is way less dramatic than a spaghetti bolognese with no garlic bread.

"What did she do, then?" she asks.

I glance at Joe. It doesn't *look* like he's listening as he looks out of the car window, but I don't want to give him anything more to worry about. And anyway, it really is just that Barbara was annoying. I mean, she carried my bag and escorted me around, exactly as she's meant to. I can't exactly complain that she was *too* helpful, can I?

"Nothing much." I shrug. "She was just a bit keen. No big deal."

"Oh." Mum pulls into McDonald's. "OK. Well, you know how it can be. It might take a day or two to get used to each other."

"Yeah. Probably," I agree. I really hope that Mum's right.

We all walk into McDonald's, ready to get *noticed*. But the restaurant's fairly quiet and we manage to find ourselves a nice table in the corner before too many people spot us.

I wait until everyone has given Dad their order and

63

Joe's busy colouring and then I slide up towards Mum, ready to talk to her about the audition.

"So, Mum," I start. "You remember the Fusion concert?"

"Well, yes, Erin, it was last week." Mum's eyes narrow.

"I've had that 'Love My Life' in my head ever since." Nanny starts swaying and humming. "Such a catchy tune."

"Well..." I meet Aimee's eyes as she gives me an encouraging nod. "Do you remember they said they're looking for girls to audition to form Fusion Junior?"

"Uh-huh." Mum looks a bit suspicious as Nanny stops humming.

"I always wanted to be in a pop group," Nanny muses as she gives my hand a friendly pat. "But after winning the top prize for the largest pumpkin at the Dundonald Fair, you quickly learn that fame isn't all it's cracked up to be." She shakes her head seriously.

"Well, actually..."

"*No*, Erin." Mum interrupts me with a firm shake of her head. "I know what you're about to say, but you've only just started at All Saints. I think that's tiring enough. The last thing you need is to be applying for a junior pop group, even if it is Fusion. And anyway, I thought you'd decided that you didn't want to perform any more? What's changed?"

"Well, that's my fault. . ." Aimee jumps in before I have a chance to answer. "*I* suggested it. I just thought it might be a bit of fun?" She shrugs hopefully. "And you never know, maybe Erin could actually get into Fusion Junior? That would be so great, wouldn't it?"

"Erin will get in." Joe looks up from his colouring with a huge smile on his face. "Erin's definitely going to be in Fusion Junior."

"Aw." Mum, Nanny and Aimee all look at Joe, their hands to their chest, as I pretend I have no idea why he just said that.

"You should let her have a try." Nanny pats Mum's arm. "Where's the harm?"

"I don't know," Mum sighs as she gives her pregnant belly a rub. Mum has started rubbing her belly when she's feeling *protective*. "I'm just not sure if. . ." She stops talking mid-sentence as a group of teenagers walk into McDonald's. Her eyes meet with Dad's at the till as they share *the look*. The one that they always share when we're out. The one that says that we might be about to get some *unwanted attention*. The teenagers are really loud and chatty, but they don't actually seem to notice us at all. One of them stops and looks our way and I feel Mum tense as she moves to block Joe from sight. But then he just turns away and gets in the queue with his friends. "Anyway," she carries on talking, still keeping a watchful eye on them, hand still rubbing her belly, "I'm just not sure if this is the right time to be thinking about auditioning for Fusion Junior."

"But Mum. . ." I give her a pleading look.

"Oh, give her a chance, love." Nanny interrupts. "It'll be good for her."

I see Mum tense again and I turn back towards the teenagers. But they've actually gone and sat down and they're not paying us any attention at all. They're having a laugh and a giggle at something completely different.

But then I see why Mum's tensed.

There's a lady behind us. She has her back to us, but over her shoulder her phone is secretly pointing towards us.

A Secret Photographer.

Dad saunters over from the counter, carrying a tray full of our McDonald's orders, a big dopey grin on his face.

"So, who ordered chicken nuggets?" He stands between the camera and us really casually, as if he totally hasn't noticed her, and starts dishing out our food, blocking us from view, just like he always does when this happens.

He doesn't sit down to eat, and I know that Dad will eat the rest of his McDonald's standing up in that exact position. Blocking the lady from taking our photo and pretending that he stands up to eat in McDonald's all the time, when we know exactly why he's standing there. Well, except for Joe, anyway. He just munches away on his Happy Meal.

"We're *always* in the spotlight, Erin," Mum rubs her forehead. "Do you really want *more* of this?" She gestures back towards the lady with the camera over her shoulder.

"Mum." I look her right in the eyes. "I *really* want to do this." I glance at Joe. "I *need* to."

Mum and Dad share a look and I hold my breath as I wait for them to decide.

"Just don't let it take too much attention away from your schoolwork, OK?" She opens her eyes wide to let me know that she *totally* means it.

"Yes, definitely, I won't!" I beam.

"All right, then." She finally agrees.

CHAPTER 9

As soon as we get back from McDonald's, Aimee downloads "Together" on to my phone and tells me that I've got until Saturday to learn it.

"Let's record you singing it this weekend," she hands me her fluffy dog-shaped headphones, "then we can start thinking about the dance bit." She opens the back door, ready to head home, but then turns back towards me, her head tilted to one side. "You'll be OK to sing it in front of *me*, won't you? Well, me and my phone camera, anyway."

"Yeah, course." I laugh.

So, for the rest of the week, I listen to "Together", humming along with the words everywhere I go.

Well, everywhere except for my lessons, that is, seeing as I've promised Mum and Dad that I'll focus on my schoolwork. And actually, it turns out that focusing on my schoolwork isn't as tricky as I'd thought. I mean, there's a *lot* going on with it being the first week of starting at senior school.

On Tuesday morning, Miss Wilson starts us with a "getting to know each other" exercise. She tells us that as she calls our name for the register, we have to stand up and give an interesting fact about ourselves.

Aimee groans beside me, because she's one of the first on the register and she hates speaking up in class. But she actually does OK. When her name gets called, she stands up and tells everyone about her dog-walking business and how she's already saving up for fashion school; she sounds super cool, so I give her a little thumbs up as she sits down.

Next is Morgan, and she talks about how much she loves basketball and how she's planning to join the school basketball team this year.

Sophia tells us that she can do a somersault into the splits.

Isla talks about how her dad used to be in a band that had a Christmas number-one hit with "Flirty Turkey".

I'm the last one on the register and by the time it gets to me, everyone's starting to look a little bit bored, so I decide to keep mine really short.

But as I stand up, everyone stops fidgeting and the

room goes a bit quieter than it was a second ago. Barbara obviously notices the change too. She stands up next to me, puts her hand on my shoulder and tells me, just loud enough for most of the class to hear, that she's here if I need her.

Then she crosses her arms and looks threateningly at all of my classmates, and I can't help thinking again that sometimes Barbara seems more like a bodyguard than a class helper. I picture her walking along beside me, wearing a black suit and dark glasses, carrying a taser in her inside pocket and growling at anyone who so much as looks at me.

I blink as I realize that everyone in class is waiting politely for my interesting fact about myself. They probably think that I haven't spoken right away because I'm nervous, rather than because I'm daydreaming about Barbara as my bodyguard making a running leap on to Isla.

They're obviously expecting me to talk about achondroplasia, but I've already decided what I'm going to say, so I stick to the plan.

"Hi, everyone." I smile. "My name's Erin and I really love singing. I don't often sing in front of people, but I'm working on that." I go to sit back down, then hesitate as

I realize that they're all waiting for me to say something *more*, and I can't help wondering what it is they want to hear. So, even though I wasn't exactly planning to, I carry on. "Does anyone have anything that they'd like to *ask* me?" I try to ignore Barbara as she gasps and puts her hand to her chest, and I look at Miss Wilson as the room goes *even* quieter. "I don't mind answering questions about achondroplasia." I shrug. "If there are any?"

"Thank you, Erin." Miss Wilson gives me an approving nod, then looks around the class. "Does anyone have anything that they'd like to ask?" Her eyes scan the room as a couple of hands go up hesitantly.

Grace is the first.

"Ummm, so you say achon-dro-play-sia?" She tries to sound out the word. "But why don't you just say dwarfism? Is it offensive?"

"No, not at all." I laugh. "To be honest, I say dwarfism most of the time, because nobody really knows what I'm talking about when I say achondroplasia." Grace giggles. "Achondroplasia is the type of dwarfism that I have and it's the most common type. But there are a lot of different types, about two hundred altogether."

A few more hands go up now.

"Is it hard to find clothes that fit you?" asks Michelle.

"Not when you have a best friend who can sew like Aimee can." I laugh and a few girls in the class laugh along with me. "There aren't all that many places that sell clothes especially for little people." I shrug. "So, it can be a bit tricky." I pull at my blazer. "My nan had to buy six sizes of this blazer just so that she could find the best one to adjust."

"Can you still do sports?" comes the next question as more and more hands go up.

"Yeah, course!" I giggle. "I can still do anything that an average-sized person can do. Just, sometimes in a different way. So, I guess for some sports I might need slightly different equipment. Like, a shorter hockey stick or a bench to stand on if I was going to be shooting hoops in basketball." I smile at Morgan.

"OK, I think we've got time for one more question." Miss Wilson scans the room, until finally her eyes rest on Isla and she gives her a look to let her know that she can go next.

"Well, it's not really to do with dwarfism." Isla looks all around the class wide-eyed as she twizzles her ponytail between her fingers. "But I'd just *love* to hear Erin sing."

"Oh." My stomach drops as I hear everyone in class murmuring in agreement. *"Really?"* But then I remember the line on the *Fusion Junior Audition To-Do List*. The one that says, *Practise singing in public*.

"Yes, *please*." Isla leans on her desk, rests her chin on her hand and flutters her eyelashes innocently.

I hesitate. I really don't want to sing to my class in the middle of form time. But then, I've got to be able to sing in public if I'm going to keep my promise to Joe.

"I don't think so." Miss Wilson steps forward, but before she has a chance to say anything more, I look Isla right in the eyes and I say with a confidence that I really don't feel:

"All right, then."

"Oh." Miss Wilson looks slightly taken aback. She hovers for a second as if she can't decide whether to stop me from jumping off a cliff, but then she nods uncertainly, steps to one side and signals for me to jump.

I take a deep breath as I meet Aimee's eyes. She looks so serious and unsure, and I just know that she's holding her breath right now, because she really doesn't know what's about to happen next.

I plaster a smile on my face, take a deep breath, open my mouth and. . .

Driiiing driiiiing.

The bell for first lesson rings.

"Sorry, girls!" Miss Wilson claps her hands, clearly slightly relieved that my cliff jump has been postponed for now. "We'll have to pick this up another time." She puts her hand on my shoulder. "But, well done." She leans down towards me. "And thank you."

CHAPTER 10

"Were you *seriously* about to sing?" Aimee asks me as we walk together down the PE corridor, Barbara trailing along behind us.

"I *think* so." I frown.

"Which song?" she asks. "Not 'Together'?"

"No, I'm still learning it!" I tap on Aimee's fluffy headphones. "Probably just 'Love My Life'." I smile as Aimee sidles in towards me.

"I'd love to have seen Isla's face if you'd actually got to sing. She'd have regretted asking to hear you once she'd heard how much better you are than her." She gives my arm a friendly pat. "Will you be my partner in PE today? Seeing as it's our *only* class together."

"Definitely!" I agree as we walk towards the PE changing rooms. "It's nice that your mum changed her shifts to be home more for your first week of school, but I've hardly seen you all week!"

"I might not be over much next week either," Aimee says. "I'm walking two more dogs starting next week."

"Oh." My face drops.

"Don't worry." Aimee grins. "You'll still see plenty of me."

PE doesn't go exactly as planned.

Miss Ryan, our new PE teacher, comes in and introduces herself and gives us a quick tour of the sports facilities.

It's properly huge and also amazing.

There's a sports hall, a gym hall, a swimming pool, outdoor tennis courts and even a basketball court. Our primary school literally had a playground, a field and the hall, which quadrupled up for assemblies, dinner, Christmas plays and very occasional sports.

This is a *billion* times better.

At the end of the tour, Miss Ryan gets us all to stand in a line in the basketball court and hands each of us a basketball from a bag.

I actually love basketball. I compete in a basketball team every year at the Dwarf Sports Association games.

It's this really fun Olympics-type event for anyone who has dwarfism, and it's so much fun because you get to compete in sports at an equal level. Basketball is my favourite event of the whole thing. But that's when I'm playing with people the same height as me. I've never played against average-sized people before, so I'm not exactly sure how that will go. When I had PE lessons at primary school, I was always given a slight advantage, to allow for my height disadvantage – things like running shorter distances or giving me a bit more time to rest. At the very least, my teacher would always tell me that I could do alternative exercises when I needed to. But Miss Ryan doesn't really seem to have thought of that. In fact, she doesn't make any reference to my height at all, which is kind of unusual. She asks if there's anyone who's played basketball before, so I put my hand up, but I can't help noticing that Morgan and I are the *only* ones who have our hands up. Miss Ryan smiles at us both, then asks us to stand in front of everyone so that we can demonstrate today's exercise.

I walk slowly to the front of the class with Morgan. I *really* wish that I hadn't put my hand up.

"OK?" Miss Ryan stands in front of us both and I try to look more confident than I'm feeling, even though all I want to do is run off the basketball court. But I guess that would be even more embarrassing than whatever's about to happen next, so I just stand there, fidgeting a bit and looking nervous. "How's your dribbling?"

Dribbling in basketball is basically where you bounce the ball over and over around the court, and I'm actually quite good at it. The trick is just not to let the ball bounce too far away from you. Morgan nods really enthusiastically and says that she *loves* dribbling, so I just shrug and tilt my head to the side to let Miss Ryan know that I'm not *too* bad, even though I have no idea how I compare to Morgan. "Great." Miss Ryan beams. "So, could you do a lap of the court and show the class your best dribbling, then?"

Morgan and I walk around the court bouncing the ball over and over and over, neither of us losing it once.

"Wow, you're really good!" Morgan exclaims as we get back to the front of the class.

"Yes, that was excellent," Miss Ryan agrees. "Morgan and Erin, I think you two should remain a pair for now."

I give Aimee a bit of a sorry look.

"Everyone else, into pairs. I'd like you all to practise dribbling from one cone to the other for the rest of class."

"I really hope we can partner up together next time we have PE," Aimee huffs as we get changed out of our kit at the end of the lesson. "We hardly get to see each other as it is. It would be nice if we could actually be together for the *one* class we *do* have."

"Hey, Erin!" Morgan walks towards us. "Have you thought about joining the year group basketball team? You were *so* great today."

"Errr. Not really." I shake my head as Aimee suddenly gets super focused on finding something in her bag.

"You should really think about it." Morgan points to a noticeboard in the corner of the changing rooms. "There's a sign-up sheet just there."

"Thanks." I glance towards it as if I might consider signing up, even though I totally won't. I mean, OK, so my dribbling's quite good, but playing an *actual* game of basketball in competition with girls almost *twice* my size?

I don't think so.

"You're already making *loads* of other friends." Aimee stares after Morgan with a sigh as she heads back to her locker.

"No one as good as you, Aims." I put my hand on her arm. "I really wish we were in more classes together."

"Me too." Aimee cheers up a bit.

"Good job we've got this weekend!" I grin. "I can't wait to get started on the audition video." I walk towards my locker to put my PE kit away, but as I'm tucking my bag inside, I overhear Isla and Sophia whispering from the other side of the lockers.

"Do we *really* need to practise *every* lunchtime, Isla?" Sophia asks.

"Definitely," Isla replies. "We don't have long to make this audition video. My mum says it has to be *perfect*."

Wait a minute.

They're talking about the audition video.

But are they seriously planning on practising *every day*?

I know I probably shouldn't keep listening, but I can't help hovering there just a little bit longer.

"Didn't you say that your mum knows someone who works with Fusion?" I hear Sophia say. "We've already got a better chance than *most* people. I mean, that's how you got onstage at the concert, isn't it?"

"Shhhh!" Isla hisses, and even though she couldn't know I'm here, I duck back a bit in case she looks around the corner. "Do you think you could shout it any louder?" she snaps. "And anyway, they've said the video still has to be good enough. They can't just dish out freebies to people with no *actual* talent."

I notice there's a small hole in the back of my locker.

If I stand in the right position, I can just about see them talking. I watch as Isla smooths down her blazer carefully and slowly, like she's about to say something *really* important. Then she raises her eyebrows in this excited way and says, "My mum's actually booked a video producer for us."

What? My jaw drops open.

All of a sudden, my plans with Aimee this weekend don't seem professional enough *at all*. How can we compete with *that*?

"Seriously?" Sophia's voice goes a little bit squealy.

"Yeah." Isla pulls a bright red notebook out of her bag. "We need to make sure we're *totally* ready. She's booked the video producer for the weekend of the deadline. That gives us just under three weeks to learn the dance steps *inside out*." She holds the book up towards Sophia and as it passes my spy hole I get the tiniest glimpse of a list written out with neat tick boxes next to each item. I've got to admit it looks a bit more pro than ours and I can guarantee it won't say *Practise singing in public* or *Come up with dance routine*.

"What about the singing?" Sophia asks. "You know I can't sing that well."

"Don't worry. I bet my mum can do something about

that with our home recording studio." Isla shakes her head. "Maybe we should go shopping this weekend and look at outfits. I think we should be matching. Don't you?"

"Definitely," Sophia agrees.

"And I'll get my mum to book us in for a makeover at Glow You for the day of the video shoot."

"Great," Sophia replies breathlessly.

"That just leaves the setting." Isla frowns. "It needs to be something special. Something that *no one* else will be using. Something that makes us *really* stand out."

They both stand there for a minute, neither of them saying anything as they think about where they could do the audition video, and I hold in a sigh.

How am I *ever* going to have a hope against them? I mean, I don't have a professional video producer, and I definitely don't have a home recording studio, and I'm not sure if Mum would even *let* me go for a makeover. I know getting into Fusion Junior was a long shot, but all of a sudden it feels totally *hopeless*. I start to imagine telling Joe that I can't keep my promise to him. I picture the look on his face and my heart sinks.

But then I hear Isla say, "The Observatory at the Grand Central would have been *so* perfect. My mum called them to ask, but they've told her it's not an option."

My heart picks up speed. Did she just say the *Grand Central Hotel*? The same one that Dad works at?

I shut my locker door. It might not be an option for Isla, but it could be for *me*.

Maybe it's not so hopeless after all.

"Ready for lunch, Erin?" Aimee asks from behind me.

"Yep." I cast a glance back at my locker and grin. "Let's go."

CHAPTER 11

"No way!" Aimee practically spits her chip out when I tell her about the conversation that I overheard as we sit at the lunch table. "It sounds like Isla's taking this audition video way too seriously." She picks up another chip. "I mean, if you're good enough for Fusion Junior, then it's not about how fancy the video is, it's just about showing them your natural talent, isn't it?"

"I guess." I push a pea around my plate with my fork. I don't want to disagree with Aimee, but I'm not sure that she's right on this. Isla and Sophia are just giving themselves the best possible chance, aren't they? Isn't that a good thing?

"They were talking about needing a really good setting for their video," I plough on. "They want to use the Observatory at the Grand Central, but apparently they've been turned down."

"Isn't that where your dad works?" Aimee asks.

"Uh-huh." I beam. "And I was thinking: maybe I could ask him if *we* could record *our* video there!"

"Oh." Aimee pauses, the chip halfway to her mouth. *"Really?"*

"Yep!" I widen my eyes enthusiastically. "We're going there next weekend for Nanny's birthday. I thought I could ask him about it then. I was thinking I could ask about a professional makeover too."

"A professional *makeover?*" Aimee repeats, a little taken aback. "Do you really think we need one?" Aimee isn't really a professional makeover kind of girl. "And anyway, I thought we were going to film the audition video *this* weekend?"

"I just. . ." I avoid Aimee's eyes as I concentrate on spearing the pea. "Well, I *do* want to give myself the best possible chance, and Isla seems *so* organized, and anyway, I thought a makeover might be fun."

I look up as Aimee's eyes soften.

"Trust me, Erin. You really don't need to worry about *any* of that stuff." She shakes her head. "You've got more talent in your little finger than Isla Walsh has in her whole body. I'm your creative director, remember? And I've had loads of ideas. Your video will show off exactly who you are. Fusion are going to *love* it."

I smile and let my shoulders drop as I try to shake off my doubts.

But a little voice inside my head can't help wondering if that's really going to be enough. Especially if I'm going to keep my promise to Joe.

When Saturday finally arrives, I am so excited about getting started on the audition video.

Aimee turns up at exactly 10 a.m., Rocket by her side, a small bag in her hand.

"You're looking after Rocket again?" I ask as Rocket starts sniffing Dad's roses suspiciously.

"Yep. Every Saturday now," Aimee replies as she follows me up to my room.

I walk straight to my desk and hold up a new notebook with a flourish.

"I know we already made a to-do list." I open it up to reveal a brand-new list. "But I thought I'd update it a bit."

FUSION JUNIOR AUDITION TO-DO LIST

Learn "Together"
Hair
Outfit
Makeover
Record Erin singing "Together"
Dance video music
Dance routine
Setting
Record dance video

"Oooh, fancy." Aimee giggles as she looks at the first line. "So, you've learnt 'Together', right?"

"Of course I have!" I hand Aimee back her fluffy dog-shaped earphones as she puts a big tick next to *Learn "Together"*. We both look at the next item on the to-do list: *Hair*.

"Well, then." Aimee stands behind me and puts on this funny voice, as if she's a hairdresser, as she meets my eyes in the mirror. "What are we doing with your hair today, young lady?"

Aimee's pretty sensible most of the time, so I properly love it when she gets a bit silly.

"I think. . ." I grin. "We should go *big*." I shake my head about until my hair goes massive and fabulous and Aimee leans over to my notepad and ticks hair off the list with a big flourish.

"Now for the outfit." She opens her bag and pulls out my denim jacket and I gasp because *it's amazing!* She's obviously raided Nanny's beads and buttons box again, and she's sewn the words *The Jam* on to the back of it.

"You know, because you're the jam and I'm the cheese?" Her eyes dart up for a minute, then she looks back down at the jacket. "And also, because *this*, I mean, singing and performing, well, it's *your jam*, isn't it?" She lays it down on my bed, then meets my eyes nervously. "Do you like it?"

"I *LOVE* it!" I squeal as I pick it up and hold it in front of me to admire it properly. "Thank you, Aimee, it's so class!"

"I think you should just wear a black vest and leggings with it." Aimee pulls a pair of black leggings and a vest out of my drawer. "It will look so cool with your trainers. Like you're not trying too hard. But also, that you're proud of who you are."

"It's class." I beam as I open the notepad and put another big, flourishing tick next to *Outfit*.

"Makeover." I read the next item on the list out loud, then hesitate as I remember Aimee saying that we don't need one.

"I wouldn't worry too much about a makeover." Aimee studies me in the mirror. "Your skin is incredible. I guess you could put on a bit of mascara, but Fusion probably aren't looking for someone who needs to hide behind loads of make-up anyway." She takes a folded tripod out of her bag and starts setting it up. "So, are you ready to do the singing bit?" She directs me to sit on my bed, then pulls a pair of headphones with this little microphone stick attached to them out of her bag as I climb up. "I know we don't have a home recording studio, but I thought these might improve the sound quality a bit." She puts them over my head and pulls the microphone in front of my mouth. "They're my dad's. He uses them for Zoom calls." She plugs them into her phone. "I'll play the backing track on my phone so that you can hear it on the headphones and then the microphone will pick up your voice for the recording. Does that sound OK?"

"So, we're just going to do it *right now*?" I fidget a bit as Aimee takes her position behind the tripod and fiddles about with the position of the phone.

"I think so, don't you?" She looks up. "Better to just rip

the plaster off, right?" Her hand hovers over the record button. "Just tell me when to hit play." I take a deep breath and give her a nervous nod.

She presses play and the music starts in the headphones. I've listened to this song so many times I know exactly when to start singing. It starts with this musical intro that's really soft and mellow, and I bob my head as I picture myself standing onstage in front of a waiting crowd.

I take another deep breath, open my mouth and . . . close it again. All I can think about is how last time I was on a stage I totally blew it.

"I'm not sure if I can do this." I shake my head as Aimee's head darts out from behind the camera.

"Hey, it's OK." The music in the headphones stops and Aimee comes and sits next to me on my stripy duvet. "Of course, you can, Erin." She squeezes my hand. "What were you thinking about?"

"Nothing much," I reply. "I was just picturing myself on a stage."

"Erin!" Aimee gives me a playful smack on the arm. "No wonder you stopped!" She stands back up and walks behind the tripod. "Just pretend that I'm not here. And pretend the camera's not here. Actually, just pretend there's *nobody* here." She ducks behind the tripod. "And imagine you're singing this song to someone who *really* needs to hear it."

I concentrate as the backing track starts playing again, but this time I don't think about the stage.

This time I think about Joe.

He's been coming home from school every day this week crying.

I think of his bottom lip trembling when he gets unwanted attention, and I think of him hiding behind my legs.

I take a deep breath and . . . *I start singing.*

The song starts out really mellow and soulful. It's about three girls living separate lives, who don't believe in themselves. I picture Joe's face when that kid Alfie told him that he couldn't do kung fu and somehow, even though I know he's not even here, I sing it to Joe. As the song progresses, the tempo changes a bit, and the tone lightens and the lyrics become about the girls overcoming their problems, and I picture Joe's face if I actually got a part in Fusion Junior. I smile as I imagine him kicking Alfie's butt with his best kung fu move and then the next thing I know, I'm not picturing Joe any more, I'm picturing *me*. I start belting out the song, feeling all hopeful and happy, until finally I picture myself singing it on a stage, pouring everything into it. My eyes closed; my heart full. All of my frustrations, my fears, my hopes and my joy bursting out of my mouth and into the lyrics.

The music ends and I open my eyes as I stop singing. I'm panting.

"Phffff." I exhale as I meet Aimee's astonished eyes, her mouth hanging open. "Was that OK?"

Aimee blinks twice, then shakes her head.

"Erin, that wasn't just *OK*." Her whole faces lights up. "That was completely *brilliant*!"

CHAPTER 12

"Erin, I'm not just saying this – I really think you could be in with a chance of getting into Fusion after singing like that!" Aimee hugs me tightly, then marches to my desk and puts the biggest tick of all next to *Record Erin singing "Together"*.

"Really?" Just for a second, I allow myself the tiniest flicker of hope and it makes me so happy.

"Yeah! I mean, I knew you could sing, but I've never heard you sing like *that*. When Fusion sees that, they are going to seriously flip!" Aimee flicks her shiny brown hair out of her face as we both look down at the next item on the to-do list.

Dance video music.

"I've already had a really good idea about this." Aimee looks all excited as she takes her phone off the tripod. "I bet you that Isla and Sophia will dance to 'Love My Life', but I've been wondering about doing a mash-up to a few older songs. You know, like the ones that your nan plays sometimes when we're over there."

"You think I should dance to the songs that my *nan* plays?" I can't help making a bit of a face. "Do you really think *that's* the vibe we're going for?"

"Your nan has amazing taste in music!" Aimee flicks through her phone. "Don't rule it out right away." And she starts playing this old song called "September" by Earth, Wind & Fire, which Nanny plays all the time.

"Oooh." I start wiggling my shoulders, because I actually *love* this song. "Maybe this *would* be kind of cool."

"Exactly!" Aimee puts on another song. This time it's a song that Nanny plays by Tina Turner about rolling down a river. As soon as I hear it, I start rolling my shoulders and singing along and being really dramatic about it and it's actually so much fun.

"Come on." Aimee stands up. "Let's go in the garden and just see what we come up with."

"You don't think we need to come up with a proper routine?" I call as I follow her down the stairs.

"Not with moves like that!" Aimee laughs as she puts

on "Sweet Caroline" by Neil Diamond and we dance our way down to the garden.

It's a sunny day, which is *so* unusual for Belfast, and I can't help thinking about how amazing it would be if our video really did get me through to the next round of auditions for Fusion Junior. I've been thinking so much about how I need to do this for Joe, but what if I could really get into Fusion Junior? That would be a dream come true.

Aimee gets out her tripod again and tells me where to stand. Then she puts the music on and asks me to freestyle.

At first it feels a bit weird and embarrassing, but then I can't seem to stop myself from dancing to the music and mucking about and having a laugh. We're giggling so much, because Aimee keeps putting on these really different tracks, and each time, I try to dance in the way that the song plays. I see my electric hoverboard next to the back door, so I grab it and start dancing on that too, making an entrance past the camera and then wheeling backwards, my arms everywhere, my smile massive. I start spinning round and round, until Rocket starts chasing the hoverboard and the next thing I know I'm zipping past the camera on my hoverboard, Rocket at my heels.

It's all really funny and Aimee can't stop laughing and then Mum and Dad come out to see what's so funny and the next thing I know, Aimee's put on "Kung Fu Fighting" and Joe's dancing with me too!

It's so great to see Joe dancing and showing us his kung fu moves, because he's been so quiet this week. But he gets properly into it, showing us all his kung fu form, which he learnt at his first lesson with Liam and is basically loads of kung fu moves in a certain order. We all start learning the kung fu form from Joe and doing a bit of a routine and I'm not sure how but we seem to spend the entire afternoon listening to different music and dancing in different ways and just having fun.

"We've got *so much* footage here." Aimee turns off the video. "You're going to have the most amazing audition video that Fusion have *ever* seen! I'll edit it at home tomorrow. It's going to be *so* good! You'll love it!"

"Aimee?" I ask as she puts the lead on Rocket's collar. "Do you really think I might have a chance?"

She doesn't answer right away, just picks her bag up and throws it over her shoulder. Aimee never says things that she doesn't mean and so I think she's thinking really carefully about how to reply.

"I think you actually might." A slow smile spreads

across her face. "I thought at first that we'd just make a nice video and give it a try. But after I heard you sing today..." She shakes her head. "Erin, you're not going to believe how good you sound." She nods really enthusiastically as she heads out the back door. "They'd be completely stupid not to put you in Fusion Junior!" she calls over her shoulder.

I *really* hope she's right. I'm starting to notice that the more we do this, the more I want it.

And not just to keep my promise to Joe.

The second I get out of Pat's taxi on Monday at precisely 8.48 a.m., Aimee's waiting for me. She sent me a text last night with a billion excited emojis to say that the video's ready and she can't wait to show me. But just as she's getting out her phone, Barbara appears.

"Ready, poppet?" She pulls my bag off my shoulders.

Sorry! I mouth to Aimee as she sighs and puts her phone away.

"I'll meet you at the vending machines at break time," Aimee calls after me, and I follow Barbara inside.

The morning passes super slowly. I'm dying to see the video. After a long morning of double science, I march straight towards the vending machines where Aimee is already waiting. As soon as she sees me, she runs over, her phone in her hand.

"You're going to *love* this." She holds the phone up in front of my face, puts her fluffy dog earphones on my head and presses play as I look at the screen.

The video starts with a black screen and the words: *Erin Woods, Fusion Junior Audition Video.*

Then the next thing you see is this close-up of my face looking really nervous.

The music starts playing and there's the lovely mellow intro and then I watch the screen as I take a deep breath and start *singing*.

"Have you . . . improved the sound quality?" I look up, because I've got to admit that even *I* think I sound quite good.

"Nope." Aimee grins with this massive *I told you so* look on her face.

As the song comes to an end, Aimee's kept the bit where I open my eyes and ask if it was OK, and I actually quite like it, because it's like the second I stop singing, I'm just . . . well . . . me again really.

Next, the screen goes dark, and my garden comes into view as this dramatic music starts to play.

I frown. I don't remember dancing to this music *at all*.

It's like that classical music that you get in really epic films, and I'm not sure where Aimee's going with this. I'm starting to wonder if this is even the right video and whether I should say something when I appear from one side of the screen, rolling backwards on my hoverboard, with my arms shimmying out in front of me, pouting.

It's properly funny, especially after I've just been singing all super soulfully, and I laugh so hard.

The music changes to Tina Turner's "Proud Mary" and then I roll backwards and start singing into the camera and twirling round and round on my hoverboard, looking like I'm having the best day of my entire life. The rest of the video is just as brilliant. Aimee's mixed the music so that there are little clips of all of the songs that we were dancing to and each time, it has me dancing to it in exactly the right way for the music. I didn't even know I'd been doing that! But Aimee has captured all of it and it's *so good*! She's even got my kung fu kicks in perfect time with "Kung Fu Fighting". It ends with a funny clip of me trying to get away from Rocket with that music you sometimes hear in old cartoons when there's a chase scene.

"It's amazing, Aims!" I squeal as I play it again from the beginning and giggle at all of the right bits. Aimee has done such a great job with this. It's funny and cool and—

"Aw, *so* cute." A voice speaks from over my head and Isla snatches the phone out of my hand.

CHAPTER 13

"Hey!" I reach for the phone as Isla pulls it away from me, then grabs Aimee's fluffy dog headphones from my head, puts them on and starts watching the video again from the beginning as Sophia sidles in towards her to listen too. "It's not..." I jump up as Isla rolls her eyes and lifts the phone out of my reach.

I look at Aimee because *some help, please!* But then we all go a bit quiet as my face appears on the screen and Isla watches intently as she listens to me singing my heart out. My heart is beating so hard, and I can hardly bear to look, but I also can't tear my eyes away as she listens.

She doesn't react *at all*. She just watches the screen, her eyes never leaving my singing face.

"You're *actually* quite good, you know." She glances up at me, then back down to the phone.

"Really?" My whole face lights up and I share this super *pleased* look with Aimee. Even Sophia looks surprised. Because Isla Walsh *never* gives *anyone* a compliment! And if she's saying that it's *quite good*, then that must mean it's actually better than quite good!

I watch as the video moves on to the fun and the dancing and Isla's expression changes.

She goes from absolutely no expression, which I'm guessing is her impressed face, to totally superior and judgey. And then she gives this weary sigh and yawns as if she's hoping it will end soon.

"So, is this supposed to be an audition tape for Fusion Junior?" She flicks her ponytail over her shoulder and shares this smug look with Sophia as she passes me back the phone. "I *love* that you're not trying to be *too* professional. And going a bit retro with a mash-up of old songs. That's just *adorable*. I'm sure Fusion will think you're really cute." She pats me on the head.

I look down at the phone in my hand and all of a sudden, it's gone from feeling really professional and cool to feeling completely childish and ridiculous.

How could I have thought it was good enough to get me into Fusion Junior?

I hand the phone back to Aimee.

"Well, *we* love it." Aimee grips her phone tightly in her hand. "Erin doesn't need a professional video to show Fusion how good she is. She just needs to show them her talent. And this video does that perfectly."

"You're not serious, are you?" Isla laughs. "Oh. My. God. You really think that just showing a cutesy little video of Erin waving her arms around to some fun music shows her *talent*." She turns to me. "I'm sorry your best friend doesn't believe in you enough to *properly* support you. It's a shame really. If you had the right help, you might even be in with a chance."

"Of course I believe in Erin!" Aimee steps forward, her eyebrows equally as high as Isla's. "And that's exactly why I *know* this video is good enough. Right, Erin?"

I turn towards Aimee as she throws her eyes wide and nods really encouragingly for me to agree with her.

But somehow the words just won't come out.

What if it isn't good enough?

What if I let Joe down?

"Erin?" Aimee holds her phone towards me, and I can't help but notice that the confident glint in her eye has vanished. "You love this video as much as I do, right?" She gives me that wide-eyed nod again, the one that says *you need to back up your best friend right now.*

103

"Yeah, of course I do!" I bob my head up and down super enthusiastically so that Aimee can see just *how much* I love it and Aimee looks so relieved. "*But...*" Her smile drops. "Well, this was just a *trial run*, wasn't it, Aims?" I turn back to Isla. "The final video is going to be *majorly* professional."

"*What?*" Aimee's mouth falls open. "But you were just saying how amazing it is. It took me *all* weekend. I think this is *perfect* to send to Fusion."

"Well, yeah. And I *really* love it." How can I explain to Aimee without telling her about my promise to Joe? I try and open my eyes even wider, as if the amount I open my eyes expresses my love for Aimee's video. "I just... Well, this was just our first try, right? I mean, we didn't even have a proper routine." I tail off as Isla and Sophia share another smug look and try hard not to notice that Aimee looks completely crushed.

I think of Isla and Sophia's conversation that I overheard, the one where Isla was saying they couldn't find the right setting for their video. "And remember what I was saying about the setting, Aims?" I try and get her to play along.

"Well, I remember *talking* about it." Aimee looks like she's trying to figure out a tricky maths puzzle. "But I still don't see how setting your audition video at the Grand Central Hotel—"

"*The Grand Central?*" Isla interrupts, and it's kind of nice to see her smug face falter a bit. "What do you mean, *The Grand Central?*"

"Oh. My dad works there." I act as if it's really no big deal, even though I totally know that it is to Isla. "We're going to film my audition video in the Observatory. Have you heard of it? It overlooks the whole of Belfast." I spread my arms wide, as if I'm describing us shooting my video under the Hollywood sign.

"*Seriously?*" Isla doesn't look smug at all now. In fact, she looks really jealous. "But that's the *best* view in the whole of Belfast. We were told we wouldn't be allowed to film *our* video there."

"I'm just really lucky with my dad working there, I guess." I shrug as I put my arm around Aimee, pretending not to notice as she tries to shake me off a bit. "And you've already seen how good Aimee's editing skills are. Imagine what she can do with a setting like *that*."

Isla shares another look with Sophia, then she crosses her arms and gives me this appraising look, like she's a bit impressed. "You know, we really should chat more often, Erin." She glances sideways at Aimee, who has gone from crushed to fuming. Isla leans back and smiles, like *properly* smiles. "Hopefully see you soon." She flicks her hair over her shoulder and flounces off.

I turn to Aimee and breathe a sigh of relief, because I think I rescued that situation *really* well.

But Aimee has a face like thunder.

"I really do love it." I point to the phone in her hand. "But what if Isla's right? What if it isn't professional enough? I can still ask my mum about the whole makeover thing, and I can talk to my dad about using the Observatory at the Grand Central."

"I thought we'd decided that you don't need a makeover," Aimee replies a bit huffily. "And anyway, your garden was *fine*."

"I know," I say, trying to convince her. "I just *need* to give myself the best possible chance."

"Need?" Aimee crosses her arms and looks at me closely, her eyes narrowed.

"I mean, I *want* to give myself the best possible chance?" I shrug as Aimee's shoulders drop and she rolls her eyes. Should I tell her about Joe? I picture his face if I had to tell him I can't keep my promise. And knowing Aimee, she'd insist I tell him just that. No. I have to keep it to myself. And most importantly, I have to keep my promise to Joe. So, I try to think of another way to convince Aimee. "Can we just have one more try at filming? I'll talk to Dad about using the Observatory and I'll talk to Mum about booking a makeover. Then we can compare the two videos and choose which one we like the best together, *OK*?" Aimee thinks about it for a minute, so I give her my proper pleading face. "Please, Aims."

"Fine." She shakes her head. "But just so you know, *I* don't think you need this whole makeover or Grand Central thing." She holds up her phone. "I think *this* video is good enough."

But before I have a chance to say anything more, the bell rings for the end of break and I see Barbara tapping her watch as she waits to escort me to my next class.

CHAPTER 14

I don't see Aimee much at all for the next couple of days. She doesn't reply to my text asking her to come over on Monday evening. And she's not waiting for me at the school gates on Tuesday morning when I arrive at school in Pat's taxi, right at 8.48 a.m.

Instead, *Barbara* is.

Pat's obviously told her about the whole 8.48 a.m. thing, because as we pull in, she taps her watch and gives Pat this really elaborate air clap.

It's *majorly* embarrassing.

Pat absolutely loves it, of course.

In form time, when I finally see Aimee, she tells me quietly that she won't be coming over after school this week because her mum's shifts have changed. And then she says that she's asked Morgan to be my lunch buddy for the rest of the week, because she'll be going to the library *every day* to do her homework.

"Have you really got that much homework, Aims?" I can't help asking, because it's only our second week at All Saints All Girls and I haven't been given *any* homework yet.

But Aimee just looks a bit awkward. She mumbles something about getting ahead with her subjects, then starts rummaging around in her bag as if she's really busy with something.

"Is everything OK, Aims?"

Because it really doesn't feel like it.

In fact, it feels like Aimee is making excuses to avoid me.

"Just give me some time, Erin, OK?" Aimee says, still looking inside her bag.

Time? For what?

So, for the rest of the week, I "give Aimee time". Even though I can't help wondering, did I really do something bad enough to deserve all this "time"?

Because I'm not sure that I did. But I definitely don't want to argue about it.

So I don't mention the audition at all, and we just say hi politely when we see each other in form time as if nothing has happened.

Which is just weird. Because even though we haven't exactly argued, it totally feels like we have.

I've never been without Aimee before, and I find myself constantly looking out for her. And even though Morgan is a great lunch buddy, I can't help noticing that I need to tell her a bit more when I need things. Like passing me cutlery or helping me to put my tray in the trolleys after lunch or telling me what the food looks like over the counter, because chicken wrap might sound dead nice, but if it's covered in sauce, then I'm *not* going to like it.

Aimee always just knows that stuff, which makes things so much easier . . . when she's talking to me, anyway.

But it's not all bad. Morgan is nice and really easy to chat to, and I start to get to know some of the other girls in my classes too. I'm finally figuring out my way around school without using the map and Barbara seems to be getting a *bit* less annoying. She gives me a lift key of my own and stops escorting me everywhere I go, which is so much better. She actually just takes my bag to class and gets everything ready for when I arrive, rather than making a show of plumping up my pillow or asking if there's anything I need. Every time I arrive at my lesson, she's already put a stool next to my chair and a pillow on my seat. Sometimes, she even puts a glass of water on my desk, which isn't strictly necessary, but it is kind of nice.

And ... the big news: I think that Pat has a crush on her! This morning in the taxi, when he was pretending to be a millionaire and I was pretending to be a pop star, he started talking about how he was going to fly his true love in a helicopter to Paris for dinner on top of the Eiffel Tower. And then when we arrived at school, dead on 8.48 a.m., he blushed so hard when Barbara gave him his air clap.

But by the time it gets to Friday afternoon, I'm feeling like I *really* need to talk to Aimee. Joe's been coming home from school every day crying, and the only thing that distracts him seems to be either working on his kung fu form or helping me practise my dance routine for the video. I still need to talk to Dad about the Observatory and to Mum about the makeover, and I'm starting to wonder if Aimee will have stopped avoiding me by next weekend, because the Fusion deadline is coming up and there isn't time for her to stay in a mood much longer.

I try to catch her eye in PE, but Miss Ryan tells us that we're going to be practising tackling and she pairs me with Morgan and asks us to stand at the front to give a demonstration . . . again.

She passes me a ball and tells me that my job is to dribble my ball from one end of the court to the other.

Then she tells Morgan that it's her job to *stop* me.

I hold the ball in my hand, and I look up at Morgan. She's *so* tall.

"You want me to dribble the ball . . . *past* Morgan?" I look at Miss Ryan as if she's just suggested that I wrestle a bear on the basketball court.

I turn towards the line of girls watching me. They're obviously thinking the same thing. I've got *zero* chance of dribbling my ball past Morgan. She's taller than me, faster than me and has a greater reach than me.

Grace blinks twice, before giving me an unconvincing thumbs up as a few of the girls take a step backwards. Even Aimee looks a bit nervous.

But Miss Ryan doesn't seem to notice at all. She just joins the girls at the side of the court and blows her whistle for us to begin. I kind of like that Miss Ryan doesn't ever give me an advantage to make up for my height disadvantage, but seriously? How on earth am I supposed to get past Morgan?

I take a deep breath and start bouncing the ball. Then I look up as Morgan advances towards me.

I dodge to the left.

Morgan mirrors my move.

I dodge to the right.

Morgan mirrors me again.

I set my sights on the end of the basketball court.

Do I just make a run for it?

But as my eyes are on the other side of the court, Morgan lunges for the ball. She doesn't reach down far enough, and I duck to the side fairly easily.

She lunges again and I realize that actually, it's pretty hard for her to reach the ball down at my level.

"Use your strengths, Erin!" Aimee shouts from the sidelines. And suddenly I know *exactly* what I need to do.

I just need to keep the ball *low*.

I swivel to the left, I turn to the right, keeping the ball low the whole time, easily dodging Morgan's lunges. I can see Morgan getting frustrated. I mean, let's face it, this isn't how *either* of us thought this was going to go. But as we nearly reach the end of the court, Morgan plants herself square in front of me, her legs apart, her arms low, her nostrils flared.

She does *not* plan to let me get past her this time.

I look to the end of the court; it's really not far now. I take the ball even lower, bounce it *through her legs*, dart past her, catch the bounce and reach the other side of the court. All while Morgan is still looking through her legs, trying to figure out what just happened.

"Yes, Erin!" Miss Ryan shouts, and the whole class cheers.

"That was *brilliant*!" Morgan takes the ball out of my hands and I can't help grinning from ear to ear. "Are you sure you won't join the team? We could *really* use a player like you."

"Thanks." I beam a bit breathlessly.

"I mean it, Erin." Morgan puts her hand on my arm. "Think about it, yeah?"

"Errr. Yeah. Sure. I'll think about it." I shrug, even though I'm really not planning on joining the basketball team.

"Hey, if it helps to convince you, Miss Ryan was just saying that the basketball team get a day off soon. We're supposed to be helping at some primary school Winter Olympics event or something. That might be fun, right?" She wiggles her eyebrows.

"Yeah." I giggle. "A day off school does sound good right now." Morgan gives me a playful nudge on the arm, then starts chatting to Grace, just as I see Aimee out of the corner of my eye. She's been watching as I chat to

Morgan. She gives me a little wave and thumbs up, then turns away and starts walking towards the changing room. Maybe that means she's had enough "time". I tell Morgan and Grace that I'll see them later and I follow behind.

"Thanks." I put my bag down next to Aimee a couple of minutes later in the changing room. "I'd never have thought of bouncing the ball through Morgan's legs if you hadn't called out."

"No problem." Aimee gives me this really genuine smile. "You did so great."

It's a nice moment, so before I have a chance to think about it, I just say, "So, are we still on for filming at the Grand Central next weekend?" Almost as soon as the words are out of my mouth, the atmosphere gets majorly frosty. But I pretend not to notice as I carry on. "I still haven't checked with my dad, but we're going there tomorrow for Nanny's birthday so I'm going to ask him then. And having a makeover first would be really fun, wouldn't it, Aims?"

Aimee doesn't reply. She just sighs and start changing out of her PE kit as I stand there, my heart beating hard, waiting to hear what she'll say.

"I've already agreed to look after Rocket that weekend," she finally replies, still not looking up. "So I don't think I can."

"Really?" My shoulders drop. Is Aimee *seriously* not going to help me? "But..." I have no idea what to say to convince Aimee that she *has* to help me. "Please, Aims," I finally try.

"Erin!" Aimee pushes her hair out of her face as she starts stuffing her clothes into her PE bag. "I really don't think you need a makeover or the Grand Central. We've already got a great video. I thought this was just about having some fun together." She stands up to face me. "What changed?"

"I'm not sure." I sigh. "I guess I just *really* want this." I think of my promise to Joe. This would all be so much easier if she just knew about it. Maybe Aimee would understand better then. "Look, Aims..."

"Then you just need to be yourself." Aimee interrupts before I have a chance to say anything else. "Like in the video that we've *already done*." She zips up her bag. "I don't think I want to help you to be someone *different*."

"But how is using the Grand Central and getting a makeover being someone different?" I retort, all thoughts of telling her about Joe forgotten. So maybe I'm doing this for Joe, but I actually like the idea of having a makeover and filming in an amazing setting and Aimee is being *really* difficult about it. "It's just a *better* version of me, isn't it?" I stop as a few girls turn to look our way, and I try to push away all of the bad feelings that are brimming inside me. "Please, Aimee." I open my eyes really wide. "*Please* can you help me?"

Aimee picks up her bag and puts it in her locker, then turns towards me.

"Fine." She rolls her eyes. "If your dad says yes to the Grand Central, I guess I'll be there." And with that she walks out of the changing rooms, the door banging shut behind her.

CHAPTER 15

When Saturday arrives, Mum and Dad get us to dress up really smartly for the afternoon tea at the Observatory.

"No kung fu kicks today, buddy, all right?" Dad tells Joe in the car on the way to pick up Nanny as Joe tugs at his shirt collar. "This is Nanny's birthday treat, so best behaviour."

Joe nods, but he doesn't say anything.

It might be a big treat to have afternoon tea in a posh restaurant with the best views of Belfast, but we're never quite sure how people will react when our family walk into a room.

Joe gets more nervous than any of us. Especially lately.

"You don't need to worry, Joe." Dad pulls his hand gently away from his collar. "You're going to *really* love it there."

It turns out that Dad is not wrong.

As we walk into the lobby of the hotel, Mum, Joe, Nanny and I just stop and stare.

"Wow, Dad." I give him a majorly impressed face.

This place is properly *posh*.

The floors and walls are all made of marble and they're super shiny and clean.

Our footsteps seem to echo as we walk towards the lift and there's this hushed, whispery feeling, like when you walk into a library. Except this would be the world's classiest library. So classy that there probably wouldn't even be any books in it. You'd just have to sit here and be quiet and think about books.

Mum and Dad are holding hands and looking a bit mushy as we walk into the lift, and I feel Joe put his hand in mine. None of us talk much in the lift as we go up to the twenty-third floor. None of us except for Dad, anyway. He tells us how it's a special lift just for the Observatory and that it's actually the highest structure in Northern Ireland.

I try to listen. But to be honest, all I can think about is how cool my audition video will look if Dad lets me film it here.

I mean, it's *so class*.

There's a short ding at the top floor and the doors open

to reveal this completely *incredible* restaurant. There are floor-to-ceiling windows around the entire room and the view is so amazing! For a minute I completely forget that there are other people here having afternoon tea and I gasp really loudly and run to the window. I can see the Titanic Belfast and Cave Hill! I can even see the clouds rolling in over the hills just outside of Belfast.

We're escorted to an amazing table right next to the very best view, and Dad's obviously had a word with the staff, because nobody says anything or appears to notice us at all. There are even three stools next to each of our chairs. We climb on to the seats and a waiter tucks in our chairs and it's already the best restaurant experience I've ever had in my whole life.

I *really* hope Dad says yes to filming my audition video here.

"This place is so amazing." I lean in towards Dad and give him my brightest smile.

"Thank you, Erin." Dad beams. I give the restaurant another appreciative look and then I gasp as if I've literally just had an idea. "You know, it would make *such* a great setting for my Fusion audition video!"

"Oh." Dad's eyes dart around the room, like a slightly frightened buffalo who knows he's being stalked, but he's not sure where the attack is going to come from. "Really?" He picks up the menu and starts studying it *really* carefully. "Well, it's a lovely setting, to be sure."

"Don't *you* think this would be an amazing setting for my audition video, Nanny?" I give Nanny one of those really encouraging wide-eyed tilts of the head to get her to play along.

"Oh yes, definitely." Nanny follows my lead as Mum's head jerks up, her eyes narrow suspiciously. How does she *always* know when I'm up to something?

I pretend not to notice.

"*Aimee* would love it here too." I lean my chin on my hand and try to ignore the funny feeling in my belly when I think of Aimee. "Maybe I could bring her here next weekend?"

"You want to bring Aimee here *next weekend*?" Dad looks up from the menu. "We're probably fully booked next weekend, Erin."

"Oh." My smile drops.

"But I could try and arrange for the two of you to have a milkshake before we officially open in the morning."

"*Really?*" My eyes go round. "That would be amazing, Dad. And you won't mind if we make a quick video while we're here?"

"I expect that would be OK." Dad rolls his eyes, the corners of his mouth twitching. "You can come before we open, so long as you don't mind the odd staff member milling about. I'll tell them to expect you."

"That's great!" I beam. "Thanks, Dad!"

"Is there anything else you're after next weekend, Erin?" Mum crosses her arms. "An all-expenses trip to the Caribbean, maybe? Or a ride on an elephant?"

"Actually" – I lean towards her – "I'd really like a professional makeover at Glow You."

"A *makeover*?" Mum clearly regrets asking. "What do you want a *makeover* for?"

"I just thought it would be fun." I shrug. "And I've still got some birthday money left over that I could use for it."

"Tsk, Erin. We'll see." Mum gives me a look to let me know that she's not going to talk about it right now. "We're here to celebrate Nanny's birthday, not to talk about your weekend plans." She picks up her glass of lemonade and raises it towards Nanny, then puts the glass back down, fidgets a little on the seat and gives her tummy a gentle rub. Her pregnant belly is really starting to show now. It's probably a bit uncomfortable. "Not long until the twenty-week scan." Mum reaches for Dad's hand. "How's everyone feeling about that?" She looks at me and Joe as I try not to groan. Ever since Mum and Dad told us that we're going to have a little baby sister or brother, they constantly want to talk about our *feelings* about whether the baby will have achondroplasia or not. Because even though Mum, me and Joe all have achondroplasia, there's actually a 50 per cent chance that the baby could be average-sized, like Dad.

"I hope that the baby's small, like me," Joe pipes up from his chair. "Then they'll be nice. And they can be my friend."

"The baby will be nice, whatever size they are, buddy." Dad ruffles Joe's hair fondly. "And they'll definitely be your friend."

"No." Joe shakes his head. "Sometimes tall boys can be mean. I'd like the baby to be small, like me." He grabs my arm tightly. "And like Erin." He stares into my eyes with this big soppy grin on his face. "You're my best friend." He nuzzles into my arm as Mum, Dad and Nanny all watch with a sad look in their eyes.

"Of course I am, Joe." I hug him tight, wishing so much that I could make things easier for him at school. Things might be weird with Aimee right now, but maybe it's worth it if I can make Joe feel better.

"Well, we'll find out soon enough." Mum watches us

sadly. "And then we'll have a bit of time to think about it as a family before the baby arrives."

"I'd love to have a word with that boy Alfie's mother," I hear Nanny whisper to Mum.

"I've spoken to his teacher," Mum whispers back. "We're getting it sorted."

I nod, a little glassy-eyed, because all of a sudden my brain has gone into overdrive. If the new baby has dwarfism, will they need my help the way Joe does? Maybe it would be better if they're average-sized. At least then I wouldn't need to worry about them. At least then I wouldn't be making wild promises that I don't know if I can keep.

"Maybe the baby's something you could chat to Charlie, Orla and Niamh about?" Mum suggests. "I've actually invited them over tomorrow. Charlie's mum had a baby last year, so I'm sure he could talk you through it."

"Oh, OK!" I nod, because I love seeing Charlie, Orla and Niamh. I met them years ago at the Dwarf Sports Association annual games when we were on the same basketball team. They have dwarfism too and they're *so nice*. I don't have all that many friends who have achondroplasia, so our mums arrange for us to meet up every so often.

"I've noticed that Aimee hasn't been coming over so

much lately." Mum puts her hand on mine. "Is everything OK with you girls?"

"Yeah." I frown, because every time I think about Aimee, I feel a bit funny. Mum seems to notice that I feel a bit uncomfortable, so she doesn't push it. Mum's good like that. She knows when to ask me questions and when to leave me alone.

Today it's a leave-alone day.

She looks like she's thinking about saying something else, then stops and shrugs. "Maybe you could chat to Charlie, Orla and Niamh about *that* tomorrow too," she suggests.

Understandably, Joe's lost interest in the conversation. He's been trying to reach a breadstick ever since the waiter put them on the table, along with these super posh cocktail drinks that Dad's already made a start on. Joe stands on his chair and reaches right forwards to the centre of the table for the breadstick.

"Joe, no!" I cry, too late.

The table lifts a little, and our drinks all tumble, and Joe falls off his chair and on to the floor with a *thwump* and a crash.

"Joe!" Mum drops to her feet from her chair and tries to help him up as Dad and I try to ignore that the restaurant has gone quiet and that everyone is staring at us. We start mopping up the lovely cocktails with our napkins, but I can't help but peek behind us.

Everyone is still staring.

But they're not staring at me or Mum or Dad.

They're all staring at Joe. One lady turns to another and calls him a *poor wee lamb*, and then a little girl points and says he's cute.

It's Joe's worst nightmare.

He edges under the table out of sight, his bottom lip trembling, and I don't hesitate.

"Oh, silly me!" I drop down from my chair and stand right in front of Joe, looking squarely at them all. "I couldn't reach my drink." I smile and wave, just like Mum always says to do. "So sorry, everyone." I roll my eyes at myself and give a little shrug.

There's this kind of collective simper from everyone as they all mimic my shrug, then turn back to their afternoon tea.

"It's OK, Joe," I whisper as the waiters start clearing up the soggy napkins and bring us new drinks. "Nobody's looking now." Joe comes out from under the table and throws himself into my arms.

CHAPTER 16

It doesn't take too long for Joe to calm down once everyone stops looking at him and after the spilt drinks are cleared up, and then afternoon tea in the Observatory actually goes quite well. I don't think I've ever had sandwiches that nice, and those scones were properly incredible.

But the next day, I'm still thinking about the new baby, so the second Charlie, Orla and Niamh arrive, I hustle them up to my room, sit them down with a plate of Jaffa cakes, and let the questioning begin.

"What was it like when your baby brother was born last year, Charlie?" I get straight to the point as Orla studies the posters on my wall and Niamh makes herself comfortable on my desk chair, then starts flicking through my latest *Shout* magazine.

"Um." Charlie runs his hand through his scruffy brown hair as he thinks about it, then shrugs, takes a Jaffa cake from the plate and puts the whole thing in his mouth. "Not too bad," he says through his mouthful. "But he doesn't sleep much. My mum's really tired *all* the time." I wait for him to say more. He doesn't. He just stuffs another Jaffa cake in his mouth, then wipes the crumbs off his *Mandalorian* T-shirt.

"Is he. . ." I pause. "Like us?"

"Oh." Charlie's face lights up with understanding. "Oh, no." He shakes his head. "None of my brothers have dwarfism."

"Same here." Orla tosses her shiny black ponytail as she turns back from looking at my posters, before helping herself to a Jaffa cake. Orla's parents are super sporty, so she really likes coming here, because she gets Jaffa cakes instead of fruit smoothies. "My sister's quite tall, actually."

"Oh." I don't know why I've never asked them about this before. It's never seemed all that important.

"So, what's that like?" I ask now.

"Errrrr. It's OK." Charlie shrugs as if he thinks this is a bit of a pointless conversation. "They're them. I'm me."

"My sister helps me out with things sometimes." Orla

128

takes a nibble of Jaffa cake. "Our house hasn't been adapted like yours. So, I can't always reach everything, even with a stool. She passes me things. Mum says we're going to have the light switches lowered soon, so that will be good." She turns back to the wall to look more closely at my Fusion poster.

"I don't have any brothers or sisters." Niamh pushes her glasses back up her nose as she looks up from my magazine. She loves going through my magazines whenever she comes over. "Sometimes I wonder what it would be like." She shrugs, then goes back to her reading.

"It can get pretty annoying, to be honest." Charlie seems to warm to the conversation. "The worst thing is when people think I'm younger than Conor and he's only eight! So that can be really annoying."

Orla moves on from my Fusion poster to a photo of me and Joe.

"What's it like for you, with *your* brother?" she asks.

Now it's my turn to take a Jaffa cake and look thoughtful.

"It's nice that he's small too, I guess," I reply. "but Joe really hates all the attention." I think of him hiding behind my legs every time we go somewhere new, and I think of him hiding under the table in the Observatory yesterday, and then I think of my promise to him about getting into Fusion Junior. "He needs me quite a lot." I stuff the whole Jaffa cake in my mouth because I don't think I want to say the next thought that just popped into my head. That having another brother or sister who relies on me as much as Joe does could be really hard.

But Charlie, Orla and Niamh don't seem to notice that I'm holding back. In fact, Charlie raises his eyebrows and gives me a sage nod, clearly impressed at my Jaffa cake prowess, and I try to shake off the thoughts about my new baby brother or sister.

I'm sure it will all work out.

If the baby's tall, then they can help me out with stuff when they're older, and if they're small, like me, then ... well ... then I'll be there for them, just like I'm there for Joe. I get a warm feeling inside as I think of Joe, of his hugs and his giggles. Another brother or sister like Joe wouldn't be *so* bad. And maybe we could share stuff ... except for my clothes; I'm not giving them *any* of those.

"Where's Aimee today?" Charlie changes the subject as he pulls a little bag of dog treats out of his pocket. "I brought these for Rocket." Charlie loves Rocket and I think he's got a secret crush on Aimee. Last time he was here, they talked for two hours straight about dog training. It was so boring, but when Charlie left, he told his mum that it had been the best day of his *entire* life.

"I'm not sure." I shake my head. "Her dog-walking business has got majorly busy lately, so I haven't seen so much of her."

"Oh." I can't help noticing that Charlie looks a bit crushed as he slides the dog treats back into his pocket.

"Wow, this is so cool!" Orla points to my denim jacket hanging on the door of my wardrobe. The one that Aimee sewed *The Jam* on to. "Did you get it from Mini Mode Emporium? I love their clothes so much. Is this from that fashion line? You know, the one for dwarfism – She's Fierce by Cara? It doesn't look altered at all!"

"No, it's just my denim jacket." I sit down on my bed. "Actually, Aimee sewed it on there."

"Really? Wow, you're so lucky." Orla picks up the photo of me and Aimee and sighs. "I wish my friends would do stuff like that for me!"

"Actually," I say, before I have a chance to think about it. "We've had a bit of an argument." I frown because I'm not sure why I said that. I mean, we haven't *exactly* argued. Have we? But before I have a chance to take it back, Charlie's head whips towards me.

"What?" He plonks himself down on the other side of me. "Well, you need to sort that out. Aimee's *really* cool." He stares wistfully at the door, clearly hoping that if he looks for long enough, she might walk in through it.

"What happened?" Orla sits on the bed next to me and Niamh puts the magazine down to listen.

"I'm not really sure." I shake my head as my shoulders drop. "We've been working on this audition tape for Fusion Junior."

"You're making an audition tape to get into Fusion Junior?" Niamh looks really excited.

"And it's so great that you're getting back into performing." Orla smiles. "You always used to love that."

"Well, yeah. . ." I grin. "And Aimee helped me to make this amazing video. Their new song is going to be major. But then this girl at school, Isla, well, she kind of *knows* Fusion a bit, and she saw it and said my singing was good, but that there's no way the video is professional enough to get me an audition."

"Oh." Charlie, Orla and Niamh all cringe in unison, and it's kind of nice to see that they totally get my dilemma.

"So now," I continue, "I've arranged for us to make another video next weekend, and, well. . ." I sigh. "I don't think Aimee really wants to do it."

"Why not?" Charlie frowns.

"She keeps saying that the video we've done is good enough. Oh, and that I just have to *be myself*." I roll my eyes.

"Ah." Orla's eyes fill with understanding. "So, who do you think is right? Aimee or Isla?"

"Aimee, obviously." Charlie stands up on the bed to look out of my window. "Right, Erin?" He looks over his shoulder.

"I'm not sure." I think it over. "Isla can be a bit sassy, but she seems to know what she's talking about. And. . ." I hesitate. "Well, she said that if Aimee really believed in me then she'd properly support me. And it kind of feels like she's not. So . . . what does *that* mean?" I throw the question at them.

"There's no way that Aimee doesn't believe in you!" Charlie points to my denim jacket. "She made you *that*, Erin. Believe me, nobody sews beads on to a denim jacket like *that* if they're not *a hundred per cent* behind you."

"Has Aimee said she'll make the new video next weekend?" Niamh asks.

"Yeah." I shrug. "She has."

"Then don't worry." Orla smiles. "If she's agreed to

help you, then it probably doesn't mean *anything*. I bet she's just a bit annoyed that you took Isla's advice instead of hers."

"I guess." I nod, even though I'm not completely convinced.

"If you just have a laugh together, Aimee will probably be over it by the time it gets to Saturday." Charlie stands at the window, peering down at my basketball hoop.

"Yeah. Maybe," I agree. I *really* want Charlie, Orla and Niamh to be right about this, even though something in the pit of my stomach tells me that they're not. I take a deep breath and try to shake off my doubts.

Maybe I've been overthinking this.

Maybe this is just a cheese-and-jam thing.

A difference of opinion.

And that happens, right?

"So..." Charlie turns towards us from the window with a competitive raise of his eyebrows. "Who's up for a game of basketball?"

CHAPTER 17

"So, how did it go?" Mum asks as we wave off Charlie, Orla and Niamh later that day. "Did you have a good chat about *things?*" She leans in towards me as she gently rubs her tummy.

"Yeah." I look skyward as I think about it because I definitely am feeling better. But I can't help noticing that the bad feeling in the pit of my stomach is still there. "Thanks, Mum." I decide to ignore it. I'm probably just worn out after playing basketball for the last hour. "It was a really good idea to invite them over."

"I'm so pleased, Erin." Mum gives me a friendly nudge. "And you'll be pleased to know that I've booked you and Aimee in for makeovers at Glow You at the weekend."

"*Really?*" I beam.

"Yep." Mum smiles. "And Dad's arranged for you to have a milkshake in the Observatory afterwards. You've just got to be out by 11 a.m."

"That's brilliant!" I squeal. "I'll text Aimee now!"

Erin: We're on for next weekend, Aims! Mum's booked appointments at Glow You for both of us, and Dad's sorted the Observatory. Can't wait to see you!

Aimee: OK. I'll be there.

I sit in the taxi on Monday morning and read Aimee's text for the billionth time. It's really great that she'll be there on Saturday, but she sounds super unenthusiastic about it.

Where are the emojis? Where are the exclamation marks?

I sigh and put my phone away. She was probably just busy. It must be pretty tricky to text and hold a dog lead at the same time.

"So, how's the pop stardom going at the moment?" Pat asks from the driver's seat, and, for the first time, I don't really feel like playing along.

"Not that great right now, honestly, Pat." I groan.

"Fame not all it's cracked up to be?" Pat chuckles. "Getting chased by all those fans must be tough. I know what you mean; sometimes I just can't decide what to spend my next million on. Fame and fortune isn't as easy as everyone thinks!" He winks at me in the rear-view mirror, then stops as he finally realizes that I wasn't joking. "Is everything OK, Erin?" he asks.

"Yeah." I nod as I remember what Charlie said about not talking to Aimee about the audition and just making her laugh. "It will be." I try and think of something I can talk to Aimee about to make her laugh.

"Argh. Not another blessed red light!" Pat mutters, and I peer forward to see what's going on. We're stopped at a red light, two minutes from my school, and Pat is looking stressed and sweaty.

I look at the dashboard clock.

8.47 a.m.

Uh-oh.

"Don't worry, Pat." I stare hard at the clock, willing it not to change. "We can still make it."

The clock clicks to 8.48 a.m. just as the lights change. If Pat puts his foot down on the accelerator and picks up the pace, we could still make it. But of course, Pat *never* drives fast.

As we drive in through the school gates at exactly 8.50 a.m., tensions inside the taxi are running majorly high.

Barbara, waiting as always, smiles wide, points to her watch . . . and hesitates.

She's clearly not sure whether to give Pat an air clap or a disappointed sigh and she ends up giving a disappointed clap, which is probably the worst thing she could do, because Pat looks as if he might actually cry.

When I tell Aimee about it in form time afterwards, she properly laughs, and it feels so nice to make her giggle. So, I carry on doing what Charlie, Orla and Niamh suggested and focus on making Aimee laugh. I just need to make sure that we don't get the weird awkward tension again until Saturday, when the video will be finished and we can get back to just being besties.

Pat gives me plenty more material over the rest of the week.

On Tuesday, he arrives at my house five minutes earlier, and then for the entire journey to school he watches the clock the whole time, muttering and shaking his head if we reach any red lights.

We arrive at 8.45 a.m. No air clap from Barbara.

On Wednesday it's 8.47 a.m. Still no air clap.

On Thursday it's 8.46 a.m. and Pat is *fuming*.

On Friday, Pat arrives at my house wearing a shirt and tie, a bunch of roses on the passenger seat. We arrive at exactly 8.48 a.m. and Pat drives triumphantly into the school gates to Barbara's super enthusiastic air clap. He takes a deep breath, gets out of the car with the roses, gets down on one knee and . . . *asks her on a date!*

He's all flushed and nervous and Barbara is all giggly and shy and it's actually super lovely. Like watching one of those soppy romantic movies that Nanny loves so much, but for real.

"Was Pat on time today?" Aimee asks as soon as I sit next to her in registration. It's been so much fun giving her daily updates on the Pat situation.

"Yes!" I whisper excitedly. "And you won't believe what happened today." I check over my shoulder to make sure that Barbara's not listening. "Pat asked Barbara out on a *date!*"

"Aw." Aimee puts her hand to her heart.

"Erin!" Barbara hovers over my desk, her face a little red. "Stop talking, please, and pay attention." She says it really loudly and *everyone* in our form room stops talking and looks up, even Miss Wilson.

My jaw drops because I was talking really quietly,

and anyway why does Barbara think she needs to tell me to listen during *registration*? I mean, what am I supposed to listen to, everybody's *names*? But everyone's looking at me, so I just keep my head down and mumble, "Sorry."

Miss Wilson goes back to reading the register and I roll my eyes at Aimee, because that was *so* uncalled for, but Aimee just shrugs and mouths, *Maybe she's embarrassed?*

I turn towards Barbara. I don't think I said anything embarrassing, but then I look back at Aimee and she's making eyes at Barbara and giving her this super *understanding* smile. She turns back to me again and mouths, *She's nice, really.*

Which is kind of annoying.

But just then, Isla catches my eye. She gives me this sympathetic smile, nods towards Barbara and rolls her eyes, and my whole face lights up because she obviously totally gets it.

I look towards Aimee, feeling a bit vindicated, but Aimee just meets my eyes with this sad look as if I've betrayed her somehow, then starts getting something out of her bag.

I turn back towards Isla, and I smile again.

CHAPTER 18

When Saturday finally arrives, I am so excited. Not only am I going to finally record the perfect audition video, but I'm also going to spend the day with Aimee. We'll chat, and I'll make her giggle, and I'm going to make sure that we have the best day *ever*.

Mum gives us a lift to Glow You . I'm wearing my *The Jam* denim jacket; my hair is massive and fabulous and I'm feeling *really good* about today.

"Shall I come in with you and make sure there are no problems with the appointment?" Mum asks as she drops us off just around the corner.

"No thanks, Mum. We'll be grand." I open the car door.

"You're sure?" Mum looks at her watch. "I'm taking Joe to the park, so I won't be able to come back all that easily unless it's an emergency."

"Of course!" I say again. "We definitely won't need you, Mum."

"OK, then. You've got your phone? I'll pick you up at the hotel just after 11 a.m."

We get out of the car and walk round to the front of Glow You as Mum drives away. Walking inside the store is a bit like walking into the hairdresser's. There's a tall black reception desk right in front of us, a small row of chairs to one side, loads of little styling stations and shelves of different types and colours of make-up.

"Wow," I whisper as I give Aimee a massive, excited grin and try not to notice as she smiles tightly back, smoothing her hair behind her ears like she does when she feels uncomfortable. We walk to the front desk, where the reception lady, with her perfectly straight long blonde hair, is sitting looking at the computer screen through small square-framed glasses.

"Do you have an appointment?" she asks, not looking up from the screen.

"Yes," Aimee answers nervously. "Erin Woods and Aimee Dowling at 9 a.m. for two full makeovers."

The lady taps on the computer for a second, then her eyes light up and she finally turns towards Aimee.

"Ah, yes." She smiles and points towards the row of

chairs. "Do you want to take a seat until your friend arrives?"

"My friend?" Aimee looks really confused.

"Yes." The lady checks the screen, then turns back to her. "The appointment is for two makeovers?"

"Oh." Aimee doesn't know what to say as we both realize what's happened: the lady hasn't noticed me. The blooming desk is so tall that she can't even *see* me.

"Errrr." I jump and wave, but she still doesn't look down, so I stand back from the desk, which probably makes me look even smaller, and I wave again and say, "I'm *here!*"

"Oh!" She looks down over the desk, pushing her glasses up further on to her tiny nose, as if that will change the view. "Right." Her eyes grow a bit wide and panicked, as if she's hit a snag in her day and she's not really sure how to respond to it now. I raise my eyebrows and give her this slightly challenging look, because well, there's a *little person* in your waiting room, lady. It's not *that* bad.

She studies the computer again and mutters something about there not being any notes about *this*, and then she stands up and looks properly down at me from over the desk. "It says here that you're nearly twelve?" She frowns.

"Yes." I nod.

"Um. Are you sure about that, poppet?" She speaks to me in this baby voice, the one you use for really little kids. And then, worst of all, she turns to Aimee to ask her. "Is she really nearly twelve?"

"Well, errrr, yeah." Aimee is clearly feeling massively awkward about the situation and when Aimee feels awkward, she looks *so* shifty. She flushes bright red and looks at the floor and even *I* think she's lying, even though I know that she's not.

It's actually a bit annoying.

If she could just say *yes* in a really confident voice, then it would all be fine.

"I'm sure that I'm almost twelve." I speak loudly and clearly enough for me *and* Aimee.

The woman sighs and shakes her head and says, "Is your mummy here? I'll need parental approval."

I feel Aimee deflate beside me. This is *so* embarrassing.

"No. My *mum* is not here," I answer. "But she booked it for me so isn't *that* parental approval?"

But the lady's made up her mind now. "I don't think we can go ahead with your makeover without checking with her first." She gives a really firm shake of her head. "Maybe you could call her?"

I lift up my bag to take out my phone, but as I rummage around inside it, I get this sinking feeling in my belly. It's not there! I check my pockets. Nope. Not there either. I try really hard not to let my face drop as I realize that even though Mum asked about my phone, I've left it in the car! Mum will literally kill me for that. I mean, it's the one rule of being out without Mum: *never* forget your phone.

"Your mum already said that she can't come back," Aimee mutters before I have a chance to explain what's happened. "Remember? She's taking Joe to the park?"

The lady's been following our whispered conversation with this slightly smug look on her face, as if she thinks she's caught us out in a big lie fest, which she so has not.

"Erin, we should just go." Aimee whispers, obviously mortified as I nod and try hard to look like I don't care, even though this has been majorly embarrassing.

"You're so right, Aimee," I agree. "Maybe we *don't* need a makeover after all." I turn on my heel and strut towards the door with a confidence that I'm not really feeling. But as I get to the door, I can't reach the handle.

Gah! Why do door handles and locks always have to be *so* high up?

I give the door my death glare and stand to one side,

until Aimee opens it for me and we strut out together.

Well, at least *I* strut. Aimee just puts her head down and gets out of that place as quickly as she can.

We hover outside for a minute. Not quite sure what to do. Aimee looks a bit cross, and it's drizzling outside.

"So, I guess we should go straight to the Grand Central?" I shrug.

"I guess." Aimee shuffles her feet as we wait at the traffic lights. "Or. . ." She hesitates. "Maybe we could just have a look in some shops together. Get a hot chocolate? You could just submit the video that we already have and we could just hang out? We haven't done that in *ages*."

"*Forget* the *video*?" Is Aimee seriously suggesting that we don't bother doing the audition video at the Grand Central? All because of a *makeover*? "Hey, don't worry about the makeover." I put my hand on her arm. "It doesn't matter. Let's not let it ruin the day. You were right: I don't need one for the video."

"Well, if you don't need a makeover, then maybe the audition video we already did would be fine after all," she mutters.

I pretend not to hear. "And just wait till you've seen the Observatory! It's so amazing. Dad's arranged for us to have a milkshake up there too. We'll be the only ones in the restaurant, how cool is that?" She perks up a bit when I say that, and we start walking to the Grand Central together.

It's only a ten-minute walk, but it feels longer because for the first time ever I can't think of *anything* to talk to Aimee about. I don't want to bring up the makeover or the audition or even school.

"How's Rocket?" I finally ask.

"He's OK." Aimee shrugs.

We walk the rest of the way in silence.

Things pick up a bit when we arrive at the Grand Central. Aimee is massively impressed by the place and when the lift pings open at the Observatory, her jaw drops open.

"No way, Erin!" She grabs my arm, grins wide and legs it to the window to look at the view. "This place is incredible!" A few waiting staff are milling around laying tables and they look up and give us a friendly nod.

"I knew that you'd love it!" I beam as one of the waiters points to two chocolate milkshakes on a small table by the bar and nods to let me know they're for us. Aimee picks one up and passes it down to me and we both take an appreciative slurp.

"Now I see why you want to make your video here."

She looks around. "It really is a great backdrop."

And just like that the weird awkwardness has gone again, and Aimee starts chatting and getting properly involved, which makes me so happy. She sets up her phone on her tripod and checks the lighting, and by 10 a.m. we're ready to start filming.

We only need to record the dancing bit, because the singing was just a close-up of my face, and I don't think the backdrop matters for that. I've decided to use the *exact* mash-up of old songs that Aimee suggested before. Isla might have said it was retro, but I thought it was a good way to stand out.

Aimee starts the music.

My routine's actually quite similar to the one that we did in the first place. Except slightly more pro and without Rocket chasing me on the hoverboard or Joe kung fu kicking, so I think it goes *really* well.

Aimee just leaves the phone camera rolling and we do a few takes of my routine. Then, seeing as we have a little bit of extra time after missing the makeover, she suggests I do some freestyling to the same music so that she can do the cool mash-up thing, like she did before, but even better.

I feel a bit silly standing in front of the camera,

especially with the waiting staff still milling round, but then the music starts and my shoulders wiggle and before I know it, I'm just dancing and laughing and having fun.

"I think this is going to be really good, Erin." Aimee finishes off her milkshake. "I think it might be even better than the last one!" She looks a little bit sheepish as she walks towards the tripod to get her phone. The staff are starting to look keen for us to finish up, and Mum will be here in a minute to collect us.

But as Aimee pulls her phone off the tripod, her whole body stiffens, her mouth falls open and her face goes *really white*.

"What's wrong?" I ask, because judging by Aimee's face, it looks as though something *major* has happened.

"I'm so sorry, Erin." Aimee looks up from her phone. "I must have pressed the record button twice without noticing. *None of it has recorded.*"

CHAPTER 19

"*Seriously?*" I close my eyes and take a deep breath.

I don't know what to say.

I've worked so hard to get Aimee here to make this video with me. I've "given her time", and I've tried to make her laugh, and I haven't mentioned the audition for the whole of the last week, even though it's been the *only* thing that I could think about.

And now it turns out that the one thing that's let me down is *Aimee*.

I can't believe it.

We so *nearly* got the perfect take, even after the awful makeover situation. But it's all been a total waste of time. And actually, Aimee's been against making this more professional video ever since I suggested it.

Was this even an accident? Was Isla right? Would

Aimee be more supportive if she actually believed that Fusion would ever pick me?

I try to take a deep breath to calm my thoughts, but my heart is hammering and there are words bursting to come out of my mouth that I didn't even know I'd been thinking, but I know that if I say them, then it will be really, really bad. And so, all I can do is clamp my mouth shut, while inside I feel like I'm about to *explode*.

"We could try again next weekend?" Aimee gets out her dog-walking diary and starts flicking through it to see when she next has an opening. "I could do Sunday afternoon?" She looks up.

"We can only come here when it's not open." I speak through gritted teeth. "That's the whole reason we had to come so early today."

She'd know that if I'd been allowed to utter one word about the audition video for the last week without her getting in a massive *strop* about it.

"Oh." Aimee looks back at her diary and frowns. "Well, I don't think I can do the morning, not unless I move Rambo to the afternoon. I can call his owner and let you know?"

I can't speak.

The volcano inside my mouth is seriously threatening

to erupt. I can see the staff hovering about, waiting for us to leave. There'll be customers arriving any second, and I promised Dad that I wouldn't get in the way.

"Just forget it." I pick up my bag and march towards the fancy lift.

"Oh." Aimee trots along after me as the doors ping open and we step inside. "Well, OK. So long as you're sure? Shall we just send Fusion the first audition video we made, then? And maybe we could head to the shops now? Do you think your mum would mind? There's this new vintage shop that's opened, I thought we could..."

"Don't you even *care*?" I round on her.

And that's it.

The volcano is erupting.

There's absolutely no stopping it now. Even if I wanted to, I could not stop the red-hot lava from escaping my mouth.

"Because it doesn't feel like it!" Aimee doesn't say anything, so I keep venting. "Isla was right – if you really believed in me, then you'd support me, but instead, you're just making everything *more difficult*! Don't you even want me to get a part in Fusion Junior?"

"Of course I do!" Aimee's nostrils flare, and I instinctively take a step back. Aimee is about to have an eruption of her own. "How could you say that I don't believe in you?" Her eyes bulge out as if she literally cannot believe that I just said that. "I believe in you so much that I don't think you need a makeover or a fancy setting, because *I* think you're good enough *without it*," she hisses. "It's just window dressing, Erin. It's all the stuff people need when they're *not* good enough." She takes a deep breath, then carries on. "The problem isn't whether *I* believe in *you*. The problem is that *you* don't believe in *me*." She crosses her arms. "You haven't trusted me *at all*. Instead, you've trusted Isla! And actually, it's worse than that. It's not even that you don't believe in *me*, it's that you don't believe in *yourself*." Her voice trails off into a heartfelt sigh and all of a sudden my stomach drops quicker than the fancy lift. "You never have." She swallows hard. "It's why you freeze onstage. It's why you stopped singing in public, it's why you're getting so obsessed about making this video professional." She spits out the word *professional* as if it's something really distasteful. "And. . ." Her eyes fill with a sudden sadness. "It's why you think you need to be someone *else* to get into Fusion Junior."

"You're wrong!" My chin juts out angrily. "Of course I believe in myself! In fact, I believe in myself *so much* that I made a *promise to Joe* that I'd get into Fusion Junior!"

Aimee's mouth drops open.

"You promised Joe you'd get a part?" She gasps. "Erin, why would you do that?"

"I had to." I glare at her defiantly. "He's having a really hard time at school. I have to show him that we can be *anything*."

Aimee doesn't speak right away and we both stand in silence as the lift doors ping open.

"Erin, of course you can be anything." She reaches for my arm, her voice soft, as I step out of the lift. "But you can't make a promise like that to Joe. You have to talk to him."

"I don't need to." I yank my arm away. "Because I believe in myself so much that I'm going to make it happen. And you know what else?" I look up at her, my eyes burning. "I believe in myself so much that I believe I can do it *without you*."

"Erin. . ." She steps towards me, but it's too late.

Before she has a chance to say one more word, I turn on my heel and I walk away. I march through the fancy marble reception and straight for the doors. Thank goodness they're motion activated and I won't have to deal with a handle, because that would make the whole situation a billion times worse. I feel sick and my throat hurts because I'm trying so hard not to cry, and suddenly, I regret those words *so much*.

I never do *anything* without Aimee.

I stop and look back, just in time to see her dash into the toilets, her hands over her face.

I turn back towards the hotel doors as they open, and I look out into the drizzle outside as Mum's car drives in to pick us up, one thought still burning inside my mind.

I have to get a part in Fusion Junior.

Whether Aimee helps me or not.

CHAPTER 20

I will never get a part in Fusion Junior.

I sit in the car on the most awkward of journeys that I've ever been on, the atmosphere thicker than our milkshakes, as I realize that I have *no idea* how to do this without Aimee. And actually, now I'm in a worse position than I was when she was helping me, even if she was doing it moodily.

Because now I don't have an audition video *at all*.

And yeah, I guess I can record a new one, but I don't have the headphone microphone thing to record myself singing, I don't know how to edit videos like Aimee does, and I'm seriously running out of time.

How am I going to make a completely new video that looks even *vaguely* professional in *one week*?

It's impossible.

My stomach drops to the floor.

And how am I going to tell Joe?

Aimee mumbles that she needs to go straight home and Mum's eyes dart from Aimee to me in the rear-view mirror. Her unspoken problem alarm must be ringing louder than a foghorn.

"What happened?" she blurts the moment Aimee disappears into her house.

I meet Mum's eyes and for a second I want to tell her everything. Mum's always prepared for a situation, but then I think of my promise to Joe and I know that I can't tell her any of it.

"We just had a bit of a disagreement, Mum." The understatement of the year.

"What about?" she asks, her eyes full of concern as she parks outside our house. "Are you OK?"

"It was nothing; I'll be fine." I open the car door, let my feet drop to the ground and head straight for the back door and the biscuit tin.

I spend the rest of the weekend trying to record myself singing "Together" using my phone camera. It does not go well. None of the recordings sound as good as the one that I did with Aimee.

By Monday I'm starting to feel panicked. I haven't

managed to get a good take of my singing, I haven't figured out the whole video-editing thing, and I'm running out of time. At least Dad has said that I can film at the Observatory again next Saturday. That's the day before the closing date, so it's properly my last chance.

"Are you any good at editing videos?" I ask Barbara as she meets me that morning, a clear sign of my desperation.

"No, love." Barbara shakes her head. "Why's that? Is there anything I can help you with?"

"Not really," I mutter.

The form time awkwardness with Aimee is intense, and for the first time ever I'm happy that I don't have many classes with her.

Everyone seems to notice. It's like there's this bad smell hanging in the air between us. Anyone who walks nearby stops, makes a face that's all eyes and teeth, then backs away to safety.

It's annoying.

I mean, how can they even tell?

So, I just pretend that Aimee's not even there and that I have no idea there's any kind of atmosphere whatsoever.

Morgan sits on the other side of me, so I chat with her. It's not that hard, because Morgan is actually so easy to talk to. She tells me that her dad is from Colombia in South America and she's fluent in Spanish. It's kind of nice to talk to someone new and find out all about them. She keeps begging me to join the basketball team, and she tells me all about this professional basketball player called Hot Shot Swanson, who also has achondroplasia and plays for the Harlem Globetrotters in New York. Apparently, he's completely amazing. So I tell her that I'll have a think about joining the team, even though all I can really think about right now is the audition video.

On Tuesday morning, Joe shakes me awake before my alarm goes off.

"Erin?" He looks worried, so I pull back my covers and let him climb into my bed.

"What's up, Joe?" I ask.

He doesn't answer right away, just stays there all curled up. Eventually, he snuggle-wriggles up, until he's nose to nose with me, and then he says two words:

"Sports day."

"Oh." I nod in absolute understanding. Sports day can be the worst for us.

It can go two ways.

1. You are given an extra advantage at every event, which *seems* fair at first. But then you spend the day singled out and alone, either waiting further up the track trying to figure out if the race has started, or being given such a huge advantage that there's just no way that the average kids can beat you. So, you end up winning everything and annoying the heck out of all of your classmates.
2. You are given no advantage, lose everything and feel generally rubbish, singled out and alone.

Basically, it's pants.

Except, it's October and sports day isn't until the summer, so I don't think Joe needs to worry about it too much just yet.

"Don't worry. Sports day isn't for ages, Joe." I give him a reassuring hug.

"It's next week," Joe corrects me. "It's a Winter Olympics." He pauses. "This year, there are two sports days." He raises his eyebrows and puts two fingers up to make sure that I definitely know how many sports days that is and nods seriously. "Erin, I don't want to go."

"Oh." I sit up, because for Joe, this is *huge*.

I think about my sports days from while I was at

primary. The first year wasn't great, but the second year . . . well, Aimee made it all better.

Liam had come up with a few suggestions, like giving me a beanbag to jump over instead of a hurdle, or making the target a bit closer for throwing a ball. But Aimee made this huge list of different events that I could compete in fairly. Things like counting how many skips I could do in a minute (just with a smaller skipping rope), or how many times I could bounce a basketball. She even suggested this sport called curling, which is basically sliding a ball into a target and whoever gets the closest to the target wins.

Liam was so impressed with her ideas that he arranged for them to be included in the sports day programme. Of course, there were still some sports events that couldn't be adapted so easily, like the running races. But Aimee made those better too. She didn't leave my side. She ran with me the whole time so that I didn't feel alone. Not once.

It's actually a little bit hard thinking of all the things that made Aimee such a great friend, and I have to swallow down a lump in my throat when I realize that I won't be hanging out with her any more.

I look at Joe as he snuggles into me, and I realize that

I'm not the only one without an Aimee right now.

Joe still hasn't really made a good friend at school, and that Alfie kid's been horrid to him. I give him a hug. I guess neither of us has an Aimee in our lives at the moment.

I wish *I* could be an Aimee for Joe. If I could just be there for him. . .

I gasp as I remember that thing that Morgan said. The thing about the basketball team helping at some primary school for a Winter Olympics. It could totally be the same one! And if I was in the basketball team, then I could help too!

I smile wide because this might be a way that I can *really* help Joe. Morgan's already asked me to join the team; I just need to sign up.

"I'm going to help at your sports day, Joe." I sit up decisively. "I'll make sure that I'm there with you."

"Really?" Joe's face lights up.

"Yep." I turn back towards him. "Don't you worry, Joe, I *promise* I'll be there."

And for once I'm sure that *this* is a promise that I can actually keep.

CHAPTER 21

I have PE later that morning, so I decide to sign up for the basketball team then. But before I get a chance, Miss Ryan claps us all out of the changing rooms and on to the basketball court.

She tells us that we're going to practise our throws and then, for the first time ever, she says we can partner up with whoever we like.

It's so *typical*.

I walk towards Morgan, but she's already partnering up with Grace. In fact, everyone's getting into their partners really quickly and any second now it will only be me and Aimee left and we'll be forced to work together.

Aimee actually meets my eye. She holds my gaze for just a minute and then she starts to walk over towards me hesitantly, and I'm not sure how I feel about it. After thinking about the whole sports day thing this morning, I keep thinking about what a great friend she's always been. Maybe she's feeling as bad about our argument as I am.

"Partner with me, Erin?" Isla approaches me, her ball held out. It's more of an order than a request.

"Oh." I peek at Aimee as she jerks to a stop, her jaw clenching at the sight of Isla handing me the ball, and for a second, I think she's about to throw her ball right at Isla's head.

Except Aimee would *never* do that.

Instead, her shoulders slouch in defeat, and she turns back to the middle of the room, looking for someone else to partner with.

Isla is still waiting for me to take the ball, her eyebrows raised, daring me to turn her down. I give Aimee one last look, then sigh and turn back to Isla.

"Sure." I take the ball from her hand.

"So." Isla passes me the ball as she casts a quick glance towards Aimee. "How's your audition video going?" She gives me this smug smile, like she already knows *exactly* how my audition video is going. Horribly.

"It's *OK*. I guess." I shrug, because I don't exactly want to tell Isla that my Fusion Junior audition video is a total bust. "How about you?" I pass the ball back to her.

"It's *OK*. I guess." Isla copies my shrug.

What? My eyes narrow. Is Isla having trouble with her video too?

She puts her head to one side and raises her eyebrows really *knowingly*. "Your video isn't really going OK, is it?" She throws the ball back to me.

"Not really," I sigh as I catch the ball, then lob it back to her. I can't be bothered to keep pretending. I literally have no idea how to make a video that looks as good as the one Aimee did in the first place, let alone produce something super professional. The only thing I have now is the use of the Grand Central Hotel, which seemed so important at the time, but it's definitely not enough on its own to get me this audition!

"Ours hasn't gone great either." Isla jumps to reach the ball, then pulls it in tight towards her. "I just. . ." She looks skyward, the ball still in her hand as she thinks about it. "I don't want my audition video to be just like everyone else's. I've been trying to think of a way to stand out from the crowd." She passes the ball back to me. "So, what happened with you and Aimee, anyway?" She changes the subject as I make the catch and we both glance towards Aimee. She's had to make a three with Morgan and Grace and my stomach lurches because being the last one to find a partner is properly embarrassing and Aimee will have hated that.

It means that nobody picked her.

It means that *I* didn't pick her.

"Are you still working *together* on your audition video?" Isla interrupts my thoughts and I give a little shake of my head.

I'm not sure why, but I don't want to tell her about my argument with Aimee, so I just say, "It's not really her thing."

Isla's gaze rests on me for just a second longer than it needs to, before she moves the conversation on. "But Aimee was doing your video editing, wasn't she?"

"Yeah." I wrinkle my nose. "I'm trying to teach myself how to do it now. It's so hard!"

"My mum's hired a proper video editor for ours."

"Really?" I pretend that I don't know that.

"Uh-huh." Isla's eyes narrow. "We just haven't found the right setting yet. I'd like it to be something *really* amazing."

"That's about the only thing I have got organized." I smile as I throw the ball back to her.

"Oh yes, of course!" Isla catches it neatly. "You're doing

it in the Observatory at the Grand Central, aren't you?"

I nod and there's this silence between us. Like we're both thinking the same thing. We kind of have the answer to each other's problems. I need a video editor. Isla has one. And I have access to the Observatory. Which obviously Isla wants.

Neither of us says anything for a minute; we just pass the ball to each other with this slightly charged atmosphere. Finally, Isla pulls the ball into her chest, looks right at me and says, "We should work *together*." She says it in that same ordering voice as when she passed me the ball earlier and she throws it back to me. But this time I don't catch it.

It drops to the floor, bouncing once, then twice, then rolls to the edge of the hall.

Isla rolls her eyes and runs to get it as Aimee's head jerks towards me, like she's got some kind of spidey best friend sense that something's going on.

But all I can think is that if Isla wants to work with *me*, then maybe the audition video doesn't have to be such an impossible dream after all. Isla has a recording studio ... and a video producer ... and her mum even has contacts with Fusion.

Working with Isla would solve *all* my problems.

Maybe I don't need Aimee after all.

Isla picks up the ball from beside the wall, turns and lobs it towards me, and this time I catch it and pull it in tight.

"OK." I stand straight as I meet her eyes, the ball firmly in my hands. "Let's work together."

CHAPTER 22

The *second* that we're back in the changing rooms, Isla tells me that she's going to be taking charge of my life for the rest of the week.

"Errrrr. Riigggghhhht," is all I can say in reply as she pulls the red notebook out of her bag, scans it, then slams it shut decisively.

"If we want our dance to be any good at all, then we're going to have to practise *every* lunchtime. You'll need to bring in a packed lunch every day. There'll be no time to eat in the dinner hall."

"Right. OK." I mimic her decisive nod as I notice the basketball sign-up sheet out of the corner of my eye. I need to get signed up so that I can help at Joe's winter sports day next week. I stop as I see a note written in permanent marker at the bottom of the sign-up sheet.

First Year Basketball Selection Trials, Tuesday, 12.30 p.m.

Selection trials?

Noooooooooooooo.

"So that means..." Isla continues in her ordering voice.

"Um..." I cut her off and try to ignore how much her nose flares at my interruption. "Just a minute. I'll be right back." I dash down the line of girls changing towards Morgan as she chats to Grace a couple of benches down from me. "Morgan?" I interrupt. "What are the basketball selection trials?"

"Oh, are you signing up?" Morgan beams. "That's brilliant! Well, you're just in time. Miss Ryan's holding selection trials this lunchtime. Apparently she's actually had quite a few people sign up. But I'm sure you'll get in easily." She gives me a friendly pat on the arm. "I'll see you there."

"Great. Um, do you happen to know which primary school the team will be going to help out at?" I ask; best to be sure that it is actually for Joe's school.

Morgan squints and says, "Saint something..."

"St Winifred's?" I almost hold my breath as I wait for her to answer.

"Yes, that's it!"

"Brilliant." I breathe a sigh of relief as I turn towards the sign-up sheet at the other end of the changing rooms, where Isla is waiting for me, her arms crossed, her eyebrows raised.

"Erin, do you want to get into Fusion Junior or not?" She joins me as I stand on a bench and write my name on the basketball sign-up sheet, her foot tapping.

It's starting to feel like I'm juggling way too many Joe promises in the air.

"Yes, of course I do—" I reply as I get down from the bench.

But before I have a chance to say anything else, Isla flicks her hair over her shoulder, looks down her nose at me and says, "Then the basketball trials are *cancelled*." She yanks the pen out of my hand and raises her hand towards the sign-up sheet. "You don't have time for this today. It interrupts our rehearsal schedule."

"No. Isla." I reach for the pen a bit huffily. "I've *got* to go." I climb back up on to the bench and face her, because I *have* to do the trials, for Joe, which means that basketball today is completely *non-negotiable*. Isla's shoulders drop in surprise and her mouth forms a perfect

"O" as her hand lowers from the sign-up sheet. She is so not used to anyone saying no to her, *ever.*

"I really thought you wanted this, Erin." She composes herself. "I mean this is our *future* I'm talking about."

"I know. And I really *do.* I just *have* to do the trials. It's only for today and . . . it's for my brother."

Isla's nostrils flare as she glares down her nose at me. "Fine." She rolls her eyes as she tosses my pen on to the bench beside me. "I'll let you leave practice twenty minutes early."

"Twenty minutes!" I exclaim. "But, Isla, I have to be there at *12.30 p.m.* I'm not sure if Miss Ryan will—"

Isla doesn't let me finish. "It's the best I can offer." She pulls her bag over her shoulder. "I'll see you back here at lunchtime." She flounces out of the changing rooms, Sophia running to keep up with her.

CHAPTER 23

Audition practice *just got real*.

The very second that the lunch bell goes, Isla is standing at my desk.

"Ready?" She looks down at her watch, then passes me a protein bar. "That's your lunch today, seeing as you have to leave early. Don't say I don't care." She smiles tightly. "We'd better get going right *now*."

"Right." I look down at the protein bar in my hand, then back up at Isla as her nostrils flare intimidatingly wide. "OK," I agree. "Let's go."

Isla is an audition preparation *machine*.

She leads me into the drama studio, then gets on to the stage with Sophia, and they show me their entire dance routine.

They're dancing to "Love My Life" by Fusion, and I

can't help smiling, because Aimee was totally right when she said that's the song they'd use.

I sit on a chair and nibble my protein bar as I watch them perform their routine.

They start with their backs to me as the music begins. The song starts really slowly, and they just click their fingers in time with it. Then the music picks up tempo and they turn around really dramatically. There's a lot of hair flicking and posing, but I've got to admit, it looks sharp.

"Wow!" I say through a mouthful of protein bar after they've finished. "That was really good!"

"Thanks." Isla climbs down from the stage, all business. She takes my protein bar wrapper out of my hand as if it's some kind of biohazard, drops it on to the floor, grabs my hand and leads me on to the stage.

"I'll be in the middle," she explains as she stands me to one side. "Sophia will be on my right, seeing as she's my *right-hand girl*." Isla and Sophia share a smile as Sophia looks all pleased and pulls her ponytail over her shoulder, just like Isla does. Then Isla turns back to me, her face all serious again. "And *you'll* be on my left." She raises her eyebrows at me as if she's daring me to disagree.

"OK." I nod as Isla starts running over the routine.

There are a few moves that are a bit tricky for me. Things like leaning over a chair and holding my ponytail up high, because, well, the chairs are too tall for me to lean over, I don't actually have a ponytail to hold on to. Instead, I just end up holding a strand of my Afro and pouting, which I'm not sure is the sharp look we're going for.

"*No, Erin.*" Isla pulls my hair off my face and forces it back into a hairband. It feels weird. I *never* wear my hair up. "Have you ever thought about straightening your hair?" she asks. "I think it would probably help."

"No." I take out the hairband and give my head a shake. "I love my Afro! Can I just do something different to the ponytail thing?"

"Errr . . . *no.*" Isla rolls her eyes. "It's really important that we're all *matching.*"

I blink as I look at Erin and Sophia. Our appearances are completely opposite in almost every way. What's she on about? I'd never ask them to try and get their hair to look like mine. Because, well, it's just not possible. So what makes Isla think it's OK to say that to me?

"What about if we . . . don't match?" I suggest. "We can all just be ourselves. Shani, Robin and Brooke don't look the same. And, anyway my hair is just like Shani's."

"Erin, do you want to be in our audition video or not?" Isla huffs. "Because Sophia and I are already matching, and you need to blend in with us a little bit."

"*Blend in?*" I repeat. I've never been asked to *blend in* before. I'm not even sure if that's possible.

"Yes!" Isla's obviously finding me a bit annoying now. "You can't just *wilfully stand out* so much." She crosses her arms. "You at least need to *try*."

I almost laugh. Does Isla seriously think I *wilfully stand out*? Like she thinks I have a *choice* about it? But I don't laugh, because Isla's looking really scary right now and I can see quite far up her nostrils, so instead I just nod uncertainly and say, "I can *try*."

"Good." Isla seems a bit happier as she starts pulling my hair back into a ponytail again. "Because this is *important*, Erin. If one of us is more noticeable than the others, then we might not get judged fairly."

"OK," I say, resisting the urge to pull the hairband back out, "but I can't lean over the chair."

"No," Isla begrudgingly agrees. "We might have to do something slightly different with that bit."

We run over the routine a few times. I have ideas on how we can adapt some of the moves to suit me, and after a short while it feels like this dance might actually be quite good, after a bit of practice. But then I look at the clock and realize I need to get to the basketball trials.

"Make sure you practise at home, right?" Isla takes out her phone and pings over a video of the dance moves to me as I walk towards the door. "I want you to know the whole dance by tomorrow, so that we can start perfecting it."

"The *whole* dance by *tomorrow*?" I ask, because there are quite a few moves to learn, and I don't think that Mum will let me practise *all* night.

"Yes." Isla crosses her arms and raises her eyebrows. "Problem?"

"No, of course not." I hold my hands up. "I'll practise tonight."

"And you'd better come to my house tomorrow evening so that we can record you singing in our home recording studio. We could do a makeover while we're at it," Isla suggests as I open the door. "We probably need to look at our outfits, and we could try straightening your hair for you?"

I look at my watch; the basketball trials started ten minutes ago. I really need to go.

"OK, sure," I call over my shoulder as I leg it out of the door.

I arrive at the basketball trials fifteen minutes late, looking sweaty and worn out, and Miss Ryan is not impressed.

"I'm sorry, Erin." She shakes her head as she pulls me to one side. "I'm only looking for girls who are really committed to joining the team. I don't think that arriving fifteen minutes late shows the commitment that I want."

"I'm so sorry, miss." I give her my proper pleading face. "It won't happen again; I *really* am committed to joining the team." Miss Ryan looks me in the eye, her expression a little uncertain.

"No, I'm sorry, Erin." She shakes her head. "It doesn't give a great message to anyone who got here on time."

"Please, miss." I reach my arm out towards her as I think of Joe. "I *really* need to do this. I won't be late again. I *promise*."

I almost roll my eyes at myself. What is it with all these promises? But it seems to convince Miss Ryan.

"All right, then," she agrees. "We were actually just about to finish up with a friendly match for the last few minutes. This is your chance to prove why you should be in the squad." She stands to the side of the court. "Why don't you join Morgan's team?"

"You're here!" Morgan looks properly pleased to see me as I run over to join her. "I've been telling everyone about what a great player you are."

"Oh wow, really?" I beam, even though I feel a bit embarrassed. It's dead nice to hear that after spending the last half hour with Isla. "I hope I do all right, then." I giggle nervously.

Miss Ryan blows the whistle, and the match starts.

At first no one will pass to me. I'm standing on the edge of the court and all of the girls are just passing to each other and nobody seems to notice me standing there, waving my arms at them. But then one of the other team drops the ball and I'm *there*. I start bouncing the ball and I dribble away from them, keeping it low. None of them can get it from me, just like in PE before. I dribble all the way into their half, where Morgan is waiting. I pass her the ball . . . and she scores!

"Excellent, Erin!" Miss Ryan calls from the edge of the court as all of the other girls are giving me surprised pats on the back. "Don't underestimate Erin," Miss Ryan calls to them all, and I can't help smiling. "I'll put the team list up on Friday. And don't forget, anyone who's on the team will need to help at St Winifred's Primary

School Winter Olympics next week. Well done today!"
She meets my eye and winks, and it makes me feel so
good. So maybe I'm only trying to join the basketball
team to help at Joe's Winter Olympics, but it was actually
quite fun.

Maybe it could be fun to work with Isla and Sophia
too? If I give it a proper chance, that is.

I start running over the routine again in my head as
I walk back towards the changing rooms. Wouldn't it
be incredible if I could keep both of my promises to Joe
after all?

CHAPTER 24

On Wednesday night, Mum drives me to Isla's house. I've got to admit I'm actually a bit excited about singing in a proper recording studio, and the makeover should be fun. The audition practice was so much better today. But my feet are killing me, and I'm majorly tired. Luckily I managed to remember all of the steps today, after cramming last night and so by the end of lunchtime when we did the dance together on stage, we looked *really* sharp.

Isla even recorded us on her phone and we looked *so* good. Imagine what it will look like when the *professional* video editor gets to work on it!

As we arrive at Isla's house, there's this gated entrance leading up to a massive mansion.

"Bit fancy." Mum raises her eyebrows as she takes it

in, then looks me right in the eyes. "You've been invited here because they must like you, so you don't need to put on any airs or graces. Just remember to be yourself, OK, Erin?"

"Yeah, course." I nod as Mum presses the intercom.

"Errr . . . hello, there!" Mum speaks in this really posh voice that I've never heard her use before. "Miss Erin Woods is here to see Isla." She turns back to me as the gates open, makes a shruggy, I-don't-know-what-happened-there kind of face, and we head down the long driveway.

Isla and her mum are waiting outside for us as we pull up at the house and Isla squeals with excitement when I open the car door.

"There's our little star." Isla's mum ruffles my hair fondly as I walk past her.

"Muuuum." Isla rolls her eyes.

"Oh, I'm sorry." Her mum flushes a bit. "No offence."

"Riiigggghhhht. . ." Mum blinks twice as her head nods slowly from our car window. "I'll be back here at 8 p.m., will I? You sure you don't need me to come any earlier, Erin?"

"Oh no, definitely not." Isla's mum steps forward with this reassuring smile. "We've ordered them pizza for 7 p.m., so that's *perfection*."

"You won't recognize her after we're done with her," Isla says, giggling, as Mum's face blanches.

I give Mum a look to let her know that it's all completely fine. She mimics me a little uncertainly, before signalling for me to come to the car window and whispering really loudly, "You can call me if you need me to get you earlier."

She's being majorly *embarrassing*.

"I'll be *fine*, Mum." I roll my eyes as I half wave, half shoo her off.

She gives me another uncertain glance, closes the car window and drives slowly away.

"Sophia's already here." Isla grabs my arm and leads me inside. Her house is huge. It's a bit like walking into the Grand Central, but on a slightly smaller scale. There's marble everywhere and lots of space. It's absolutely nothing like our messy, full-up house.

"Welcome to my humble abode!" Isla spreads her arms wide.

She leads me upstairs to her bedroom, which is not actually as big as I'm expecting. Sophia's sitting on her bed reading a magazine and I peer around the room. Isla has a Fusion bedspread, a Fusion lampshade and about a hundred different Fusion posters on the wall.

"Bit of a Fusion fan?" I raise my eyebrows.

"Yeah." Isla looks all enthusiastic. "I *love* their songs so much!" She picks up her phone and puts on the latest Fusion album, then pulls out a chair from a fancy dressing table that seems to be covered in make-up and signals for me to sit down. I climb up on to it and she turns it so that I'm facing the mirror, then brings her face down so that it's next to mine. Sophia puts the magazine down and wanders over, then bends down the other side of me so that we're all locking eyes in the mirror.

I think it's supposed to be a special moment. Except, Isla keeps trying to waft my hair out of her face and then Sophia starts squeezing a spot on her chin.

"We'll start with the hair." Isla stands up. She pulls out a pair of straighteners and clicks them together. "Let's just give this a little try, shall we? You never know, you might actually love it."

"All right." I try to look more enthusiastic than I feel. My mum has always said how hard it was to find a local hairdresser for me. Although finally she found this one lady who is from Africa! She can do all sorts with my hair: braids, box braids, cornrows. I definitely don't think Isla knows how to style hair like mine. But I really want to give working with Isla and Sophia my best shot so I just shrug and say, "Let's give it a go."

An hour later and Isla looks hot and sweaty. My hair is not doing what she wants it to. It's definitely a *bit* straighter, but Isla keeps trying to straighten quite large sections of hair and I don't think the straighteners are hot enough so it kind of looks more frizzy than straight.

"I don't think this is going to work." Isla slams down the straighteners. She pulls out a brush and starts scraping my hair off my face into a really tight ponytail again. "I think we'll just have to all have our hair pulled back off our faces, like this," she decides.

"What about the ponytail pull, though?" Sophia huffs. "That's the only bit of the whole routine that I came up with."

"We could just ruffle our ponytails instead?" I suggest.

Isla looks in the mirror and gives her ponytail a pouty ruffle a couple of times.

"Yep. That works," she agrees. "Now." She claps her hands twice and Sophia and I both sit a little straighter. "On to the make-up!"

Isla and Sophia start going through all of the make-up on Isla's dressing table.

Of course, none of it is the right shade for me. I shift

uncomfortably on the chair. I so should have seen this coming.

I watch in the mirror as they meet each other's eyes and go a little bit red, then oh-so-casually put the powders and creams aside.

"I don't think I have the right shades for your skin tone," Isla explains. "Maybe you should just come to our professional makeover with us. They'll do it loads better than me anyway. Have you ever been to Glow You?"

"Err . . . yeah." I think of my last visit there. "It didn't go so well." And I tell Isla and Sophia all about it.

"There's no way that would happen if I'd have been there!" Isla gets really steamed by the story. "I can't believe Aimee didn't say something. I'd have asked to see the manager!"

"Aimee gets a bit embarrassed sometimes." I frown. I'm not sure why but I feel a bit defensive for her. "She doesn't like making a scene."

"You don't have to stick up for her with us, Erin." Isla puts her hand on my shoulder sympathetically as Sophia nods in agreement. "I can see she's really let you down."

I meet Isla's eyes in the mirror, but I don't say anything. Did Aimee really let me down? Because I've got to admit that I've been wondering if it might be the other way round. I picture her face from when I said that her video wasn't professional enough and then I remember the look in her eyes when I told her that I believed in myself so much that I could do this without her . . . and my cheeks suddenly feel hot.

"Thanks," I mumble as I look at the floor.

"Well, I won't let that happen when *we* go there." Isla shakes her head. "My mum's practically their best client. I'll get her to book us in for the morning of the video shoot." She picks up my bag and passes it to me. "So, did you bring your ideas for the audition outfit? Sophia and I were just thinking of wearing black leggings and a crop top with trainers; does that sound OK to you?"

"I had the same idea!" I beam, even though technically Aimee had the same idea, but I try not to think of that and I pull my black leggings and vest out of my bag. "And maybe this too?" I pull out my denim jacket with *The Jam* written across the back.

"Awwww. . ." Isla pulls it out of my hands and holds it up to have a good look at it. "*The Jam?* What's that about?"

"Aimee sewed that on there for me." I smile, then

hesitate. I really don't want to tell Isla about the whole cheese and jam thing. "It's just because I like singing and dancing. It's, like, *my jam*," I try to explain.

"Well, it's very sweet." Isla lays it down on her bed. "We should all have a denim jacket with something on it that describes us!"

I actually quite like that idea. I have to admit that I haven't been entirely on board with the whole total matching thing. But this is a great way for us to show our differences too.

"That's such a good idea!" Sophia agrees. "What do you think mine should say?"

We all think about it for a minute.

"Um." Isla shrugs after a moment. "We'll think of something. Erin, do you mind if I keep hold of this for now? Then I can make sure we all have matching jackets and lettering."

"Yeah, course." I watch as Isla hangs my jacket up in her wardrobe.

"Right, then." She turns back to me with this appraising look. "Ready to sing?"

CHAPTER 25

Isla leads us out of her room and along the hallway to a small lift. She raises her eyebrows as if she's about to show me something majorly impressive and presses the lift button.

It takes us down to this huge basement that's filled with musical instruments and recording equipment.

"My dad used to be in a band," Isla explains. "They actually got a Christmas number one with 'Flirty Turkey'."

"Oh yeah!" I smile. "I remember you saying in class. That's so cool."

"Uh-huh." Isla widens her eyes enthusiastically. "Except. . ." She bites her lip. "Well, none of his other songs ever made it big. We only really use the studio for me now." She walks over to a long panel that's filled with dials and lights, picks up a pair of headphones and puts them on my head. "Sophia and I have already recorded our tracks," she explains. "So, it's just you who needs to sing." She leads me into a glass-panelled room with a standing microphone in the middle of it and lowers it down to my height. "I'll play the backing track over the headphones, then you just sing into the microphone, OK?"

"Aren't you going to video me?" I ask.

"No." Isla shakes her head. "We'll record ourselves lip-syncing at the Grand Central and then the video editor will add these vocals afterwards."

"Oh." I watch as Isla and Sophia leave the room and shut the door, and I'm left standing in front of the microphone, feeling a bit nervous. "OK."

"I'm starting the backing track now," I hear through the headphones. I look out of the glass window at Isla as she speaks into a little headset, and the next thing I hear is the backing track to "Together" playing.

I take a deep breath and try to ignore that my heart is thumping really hard. This will be the first time that I've tried to sing in front of anyone other than Aimee or my family since that time onstage when I choked. I can't help thinking how weird it is that it's going to be in front of Isla Walsh, the very person who stopped me singing back then. But I'm not doing this for Isla. I'm doing this for Joe and as I think of Joe, my heart thumps just a little bit softer. I try to forget that anyone is watching me, just like Aimee said and I close my eyes and then, right on cue, I start singing.

I sing for Joe and then I sing for me. But as I belt out the chorus all about how much better things are when you're together with your friends, I sing for Aimee.

I wish she was here right now.

I open my eyes as the song finishes, take a deep breath and look up at Isla and Sophia watching through the window just outside the room.

"She's amazing," I hear Sophia's muffled whisper through the headphones.

"Shhhh! We're recording," Isla hisses as she elbows her in the ribs, before speaking to me, all business. "That's a wrap. You can come out now."

"Pizza's here!" Isla's mum's voice comes from a speaker in the ceiling, and Isla leads the way back up the lift to their dining room, where her mum's stacking a pile of encyclopaedias on a chair.

"Here you go, Erin." She stands back. "I thought this might be better for you."

"Um." My mouth opens and closes as I try to find the right words, when all I can think is has she *seriously* given me a stack of books to sit on? Because I don't want to seem ungrateful, but there's *no way* I'm sitting on a stack of books. "Um. . ." I try again. "I won't need those. Just a pillow would be fine. My back is actually the same size as an average-sized person. It's just my arms and legs that are a little shorter."

"Oh." Isla's mum goes bright red as she hastily removes the books from the chair and shoves a cushion in their place. "Sorry, Erin, I didn't realize."

"It's OK." I try not to let them see how embarrassed I feel as I climb on to the chair, my smile fixed in place. I glance towards the window. I hope Mum gets here soon. This is all getting a bit tiring.

None of us speak much as we eat the pizza.

My hair feels really uncomfortable scraped off my face and all I want to do is take off the hairband and shake it out, but instead I just nibble on my pizza and keep an ear open for Mum's car. I can't help noticing that apart from the chandelier and the posh ornaments, the dining room is completely filled with framed photos of Isla's mum and dad standing next to some really famous celebrities. There's still a bit of an awkward atmosphere in the room and I really want this to have gone well, so when we've finished eating, I try to lighten things up a bit.

"Wow, is that your mum next to Oasis?" I get down from the table and point to one of the photos.

"Yeah, it is." Isla joins me. "My mum *loves* meeting celebrities. She used to travel around with a few bands when she was younger in their tour bus." She gives the photos a dismissive wave. "That's actually how she met my dad."

I hear the sound of the front door open and close and a really tall, slightly balding man with a massive moustache, wearing beige chinos and a striped shirt, walks into the dining room carrying a golf bag.

"Oh. Hello." He stops when he sees me, clearly a little unsure about how to react.

"Dad, this is my friend Erin," Isla introduces me as I wave. Isla's dad is so not what I was expecting.

"Right." Her dad doesn't seem to know what to say at all. I guess I'm not what he was expecting either. "So, *Erin*. . ." He leans back on his heels, then forwards again. "Hmmmm, yes, well . . . you really are quite short, aren't you?" He chuckles awkwardly as I keep a polite smile fixed on my face. It's *so* annoying when people tell me I'm short, as if I hadn't noticed. Luckily, I'm saved from replying by the doorbell. Mum's arrived ten minutes early to collect me, and I'm actually really relieved.

CHAPTER 26

The next two days pass in a total blur of non-stop audition video practice, and I have to admit, I'm glad it's only going to be this intense for a couple of days. If I'm not running over my dance moves or yanking my hair in a ponytail, then I'm stuffing a protein bar in my mouth so that I can get to yet another practice with Isla.

It's exhausting.

The one time I don't think about the audition is when I go to the PE noticeboard to check if I've made it on to the basketball team. At first, as I look down the list, I don't see my name at all. But then, underneath everyone else's names, as though it's been added as a last-minute decision, my name is there, and I grin so wide.

Maybe everything's going to turn out OK after all.

When Saturday finally arrives, I'm *so* excited to finally

be filming the audition video. I'm also properly happy that it's the last time I'll have to scrape my hair right back off my face.

"Do you want me to come in this time?" Mum asks as we pull up outside Glow You. "You don't want the same thing to happen again."

"It's OK, Mum." I shake my head, even though I can't help feeling a bit nervous about coming back here. "Isla's mum will be there, and anyway, Isla said there's no way she'd let it happen again."

"All right." Mum frowns as she looks at my hair pulled back off my face. "Erin, are you sure you're happy with this whole makeover thing? You're not trying to change the way you look to fit in with these girls, are you?"

"What? Of course not!" I reply. "We just need to look the same for this video, that's all."

"Look the same?" Mum seems a little taken aback. "But Erin. . ."

"It's nothing, Mum," I interrupt her. "We're just going to match. You know, for the video?" She still doesn't look convinced. "Which will be finished today anyway," I say brightly.

"Well, all right then." Mum lets it go with a raise of her eyebrows. "So long as you're sure. I'll pick you up from the Grand Central at 11 a.m. again, right?"

"Thanks, Mum." I clamber out of the car and head towards the open door of Glow You.

"Ah, here she is!" Isla's mum beams as I walk inside. "Our little starlet." She stops, her face turning a bit pink as Isla rolls her eyes and gives her a firm nudge in the ribs. "I'm so sorry, I keep doing that, don't I?"

"It's OK." I grin as I give Isla and Sophia a wave and then I pose and give my ponytail a ruffle and a pout as they giggle. We're already wearing our black leggings and vests, and I can see Isla has a bag full of denim.

All we need now is the makeover and we're going to look *so good*.

"We're all here now," Isla's mum informs the lady behind the desk.

It's the same lady as last time I was here. Her square-framed glasses pushed on to her tiny nose, her long blonde hair perfectly straightened.

She looks over the desk and peers down at me.

"Oh." Her eyes flare wide as she recognizes me, then she sits back, her poised smile just a little bit less, well . . . *poised*. "Well, hello there." She seems to put some effort into rearranging her face, then leans forwards again, her eyes all bright and shiny as if she's never met me before and this is just the best part of her day. "I hear we're going to be giving you a makeover today?"

"Yes. That's right." I glance at Isla briefly, then look at the floor, feeling a bit hot as I remember how completely mortifying it was the last time I was here.

Isla totally notices. Her eyes flare with mischief as she turns to the lady, twizzles her ponytail slowly through her fingers and says, "Actually, Erin was here a couple of weeks ago. She got turned away by someone. I think they were really rude to her. Is that right, Erin?"

"Errrr..." I can't help the corners of my mouth twitching just a little as I watch the reception lady squirm at Isla's words. "I guess."

"Oh, really?" The lady looks all flustered and shifty. "Are you sure it was *here*?"

"Yes, definitely." Isla crosses her arms and puts her head to one side, in her best *Isla with attitude* pose and the corners of my mouth give way to a full-blown grin.

Boom. Mic drop moment for Isla.

"So I think Erin will be needing the special treatment today." Isla raises her eyebrows, and I have to admit that, even though it shouldn't be, this is just a little bit fun.

The lady at the desk sighs and blows a strand of hair from her face, then notices Isla's mum watching, quickly plasters her fake smile back on and says, "Of course."

She bends down, lifts out a box from below the desk and passes it to me. "Please accept this box of samples by way of an apology." She leans right over the desk to pass them down to me, her teeth gritted. "Now, if you could take a seat, one of our senior artists will be with you shortly."

"We will, thank you." Isla and Sophia both flick their hair and so I flick mine too, even though it's not really as flicky as theirs, and then, in perfect unison, we all turn and full-on strut to the waiting seats ... and it doesn't even matter that I have to climb up on to mine, because that was brilliant.

I imagine telling Aimee all about it. I think she'd find it funny after the last time we were here. Except ... she hates seeing people feel uncomfortable ... even mean receptionists. And she might not like it that Isla was the one who stood up for me, seeing as she probably thinks that I've chosen Isla over her. I feel this sudden heavy sadness right in the pit of my stomach as I think of Aimee.

"All OK?" Isla turns towards me.

"Yeah, of course." I answer all bright-eyed as I try and shake it off.

I don't need to be thinking about Aimee right now.

We're all called through to this nice room and introduced to our make-up artists. Mine seems so lovely. She has a big smile and an even bigger Afro, just like I have my hair most of the time, and I can't help giving my ponytail a little uncomfortable tug. It will be so nice when I can take it out later. She's laid out some make-up ready for me and I'm really pleased when I see that she already has shades that will be perfect for my skin. Isla's mum gives her instructions on how our make-up should look. I don't exactly know what she's talking about, there's a lot of talk about making our eyes *pop* and cutting the crease and root stamping and even though I know they're all just fancy make-up terms, they sound pretty terrifying, so I decide not to think on it too deeply and just let them get on with it.

An hour later and the transformation is complete. We haven't been allowed to see our faces yet and so we're all told to close our eyes and we're guided into a different room, where we stand together in front of a long mirror.

"Ready?" Isla's mum sounds really excited and I nod nervously. I can't wait to see what I look like. I really hope I like it!

"OK. Open your eyes!" Isla's mum orders, so I do and. . .

My jaw drops open.

It's me.

But it's also not me.

My eyes are all dark and smoky and my jawline is sharp. Don't get me wrong, it doesn't look bad, but with my hair pulled so tightly off my face, I look really serious and, well . . . *totally unrecognizable*.

I turn to look at Isla and Sophia and I can't help but notice that they have *exactly* the same smoky eyes and the same sharp jawline and actually, we all look *really* similar, which I'm not even sure how they've managed because normally, we're not similar in any way whatsoever.

"Take a look at Fusion Junior, girls." Isla's mum puts her hands on Isla's shoulder as she stands behind her.

"It's like I have Fusion inside me!" Sophia puts her hand to her chest as she looks all quivery.

"Well?" Isla turns towards me, her eyebrows raised. "Do you like it?"

"Errr. Yeah," I reply, even though I actually don't really know. I can't tear my eyes away from my reflection in the mirror. It's like I'm looking at somebody else, and all I can hear is Aimee's voice ringing inside my head that I think I need to be someone *else* to get into Fusion Junior.

Was she right all along?

I feel this sudden burning need to wash it all off and shake out my hair and . . . look like *me* again.

But I can't.

Today is my last chance to make the audition video.

I *have* to see it through.

As we walk through the lobby of the Grand Central Hotel, some people in reception turn and look at us. I'm used to people looking at me. But today, I feel like I'm hiding behind a mask. Like I'm saying that I'm not proud of who I am. Like I'm trying to be someone else.

Isla and Sophia absolutely love it, of course. Like their new look has given them celebrity status. They stand tall and flick their hair and they strut across the marbled lobby to the lift as I jog along beside them to keep up.

As the lift pings open at the Observatory, the cameraman's waiting for us. Dad has arranged for milkshakes to be left for us again, but Isla's mum tells us not to drink them in case they mess up our make-up.

As the cameraman sets up, Isla hands me my denim jacket, and I give a little sigh of relief. At least I'll feel like me again once I'm wearing this.

I open it to put it on . . . and my stomach hits the floor.

The words *The Jam* have been taken off!

"Isla?" I drop the jacket to the floor as if it's boiling hot, because suddenly everything feels so wrong. "Where are the words that Aimee put on it? Where's *The Jam*?"

"Oh, I cut them off." Isla picks the jacket up and hands it back to me. "I couldn't think about what to put on ours, so I just decided that we should all have a plain jacket. You don't mind, do you? I mean, you're not even friends with Aimee any more, so I didn't think that you would."

I can't speak.

My mouth opens and closes as I try to find the words.

"The letters are all in the bag." Isla huffs and gives me a look, like I'm being way too dramatic. "You can just sew them on again, if it means that much to you."

"But . . . I . . ." I stop talking, take the jacket from her, and, like a zombie, I put it on as I realize that I have made a terrible mistake.

I should never have joined up with Isla.

I should have worked it out with Aimee.

Because as I look at the letters and beads that Aimee sewed so carefully onto my denim jacket discarded in the carrier bag, I realize that unlike Isla, Aimee wanted me to be *myself* for this audition video.

And after all the time and effort and *belief* that she gave me . . . I ditched her.

Just like Isla ditched the letters on my jacket.

CHAPTER 27

The audition video goes . . . fine.

In fact, it's all over in ten minutes. We lip-sync to "Together", and then we perform the dance routine twice before the video guy, who looks a bit bored the whole time, tells us he's got all he needs and starts packing up.

It's pretty anti-climactic, actually.

All this time thinking about it, and all that practice, for just ten minutes of filming.

But at least it's finished.

I head to the toilets to wash my face and take out my hair. But the sinks are too high, and the mirrors are even higher. I can't reach the taps and I can't see myself.

I sigh.

"Are you OK?" Sophia walks out of one of the cubicles and washes her hands at the sink, then turns towards me as I just stand there looking a bit lost. She looks up at the mirrors, then back down to me and some kind of understanding passes between us. She walks towards the corner of the bathroom and pulls a really plush chair towards the mirrors for me to stand on, then opens her bag and takes out a pack of face wipes.

"Don't get me wrong, you look amazing." She passes them to me. "But you don't look like you." She shrugs and walks out of the door as I scramble on to the chair to look at myself. I pull the hairband out of my hair, shake my head and tease my Afro out with my fingers until it's big again. Then I sit down on the chair and carefully wipe my face.

When I'm done, I stand up and look in the mirror, take a deep breath and smile, feeling better already.

I climb down from the chair, walk out of the toilets, pick up my bag of discarded letters, take a glug of my milkshake and head for the lift.

"Bye, Isla." I wave as the lift pings open, but she's deep in conversation with her mum and the cameraman and none of them look up. Sophia is sitting to one side, looking a little bored as she flicks through a magazine. She glances up, meets my eyes and half-smiles, then looks back down.

I reach the lobby of the hotel. It's a little early, so I stand in the doorway and wait for Mum to arrive.

It's drizzling outside, just like last time I was here, except this time I can't see Mum's car driving in.

I sigh and look at my watch. It's only 10.45 a.m.; I've got another fifteen minutes to wait. I think about heading back up to the Observatory, but I really don't want to be around Isla or her mum right now, so I decide to just wait down here in the lobby.

Except . . . I'm on my own.

I'm *never* on my own.

I notice a few Not-So-Secret Glancers peering over at me, talking to each other behind their hands, so I go to sit in the window seat to watch for Mum.

I'm less noticeable when I'm sitting down. But then I realize that I never used the actual toilet when I washed my face upstairs and now I need a wee. I glance towards a sign pointing to the lobby toilets as I roll my eyes and shake my head.

There's no way I can use the toilet when I'm on my own. What if I got stuck inside again? I cross my legs. I'll just have to hold it until I get home.

I look out of the window and try to think of something – anything – else.

Two girls walk out of the cafe opposite, both holding a coffee, laughing and chatting, and I really wish that it was me and Aimee over there right now.

I peer over my shoulder to check behind me. If there was a secret photographer right now, I wouldn't have Dad to stand in front of me. My heart starts to pump a bit harder. Being here alone is making me feel a bit jittery.

Is this how Joe feels all the time?

Because ... well, it sucks.

Maybe it would be better if the new baby *doesn't* have achondroplasia. Then I wouldn't need to worry about them, like I worry about Joe.

"Are you OK, sweetie?" The hotel receptionist hovers over me. "Is your mummy here?" I look from her to the window just as Mum's car drives up to the front of the hotel.

Thank goodness.

"Yes, thanks." I drop down from the window seat and head out into the drizzle.

"How did it go?" Mum asks as I climb into the car. I don't answer right away, because technically speaking, it went well. The audition video is done. All we need now is for the editor to make it look all fancy and then Isla will send it off to Fusion's people.

So, why don't I feel good about it?

"It was great." I shrug as I try to shake off the weird feeling. Mum looks at me for just a little bit too long. Like she can read my mind. "It was fine, Mum. Really." I give her a look to let her know I don't want to talk about it. Mum sighs and starts driving away from the Grand Central.

Isla said that she'd email the video to me as soon as it was ready on Sunday.

She doesn't.

But even though I'm checking my email a *lot*, I don't get too worked up about it. Instead, I spend the day practising skipping, basketball bouncing and curling with Joe to get him ready for his Winter Olympics next week. When Joe thinks we've spent enough time on that, he gets me to practise his kung fu form with him. It's not a bad way to pass the time. Joe's been practising it so much and he looks amazingly cool when he does it.

I watch as the clock on the oven reaches 6 p.m.

That's it.

That's the deadline for the audition video. There's absolutely nothing more that I can do now. I feel kind of relieved. Maybe everything will go back to normal now? Except, normal used to be with Aimee. I let out a long sad breath. I'm not sure what normal will be any more.

I try to take my mind off Aimee by checking my emails again. I really was expecting to hear from Isla, even if it was just to let me know that the video had been sent off, but there's still nothing. I figure she's just busy. There's no way she'd risk not sending it on time.

On Monday morning, I get to our form room a little early so that I can ask Isla and Sophia about the audition video.

They're not there.

They run in just as the bell goes for first lesson, so there's no chance to talk to them. But I do manage to catch Isla's eye. I give her a nod and a thumbs up and whisper, "All sent?"

"Yes!" she hisses as if it's majorly annoying that I'm asking her about it. "OK?"

I guess Isla's back to her old self, then.

"Can I see it?" I whisper again.

"Erin." Barbara hovers by my desk. "We need to get to first lesson now."

"I'll email it tonight." Isla rolls her eyes.

I spend all evening checking my emails, but the only

one I get is from Mum telling me to stop checking my emails and to get on with my homework.

CHAPTER 28

On Tuesday, it's Joe's sports day, so I try and put all thoughts of the Fusion audition video to one side. It's not easy, because I'm starting to feel slightly edgy about it. Why hasn't Isla sent it to me? Is there something really wrong with it? But I can't think of *any* reason why she wouldn't let me see it. I'm probably just being paranoid.

Miss Ryan asks us to meet at Joe's school, so for once I get to travel in the car with Mum and Joe.

Mum can't stay to watch, because she's working, and I really want to make sure that Joe has a good sports day today, so I ask Miss Ryan if I can just stick with Joe, rather than being given a specific job.

She shakes her head. "No, Erin. Joe already has his class helper. You'll be on the skipping station, so maybe you can help him when he's there." I hate to disagree with Miss Ryan, but she is just plain *wrong* and clearly has *no idea* what she's talking about.

There's *no way* that Joe can manage without me.

But I don't tell Miss Ryan that. Instead I just pretend to agree, even though I've already secretly decided that if I see one tiny tremble of Joe's bottom lip, I will drop the skipping station quicker than a hot potato.

Nobody is going to stop me from being there for Joe if he needs me.

I spend the first half of the morning trying to count skips, barely concentrating, my eyes never leaving Joe as he follows the little circuit of activities with his helper, Sarah. If I see one child anywhere near him patting his head, calling him cute or saying *anything* that upsets him, I will be there like a *shot*.

I concentrate a bit more when Alfie gets to my skipping station. He's the boy who's been making things difficult for Joe. Actually, he's the boy who's been making life difficult for both of us, because if he hadn't told Joe that he was too short to do kung fu, I'd never have made that promise and I'd probably still have a best friend.

I count Alfie's skips carefully, then I halve his score and tell him he's the loser.

"You didn't count properly!" Alfie shouts at me. "I got forty-two skips. Not twenty-one!"

"Well, I'm in charge." I lean towards him, my eyes never leaving his face. "And *I* say you got twenty-one."

When Joe arrives at the skipping station, I count his skips carefully and he actually does really well.

I know I haven't been concentrating all that well, but it looks like Joe might have actually come third with sixty-three skips.

He'd only need three more and he'd be the winner. I look up at Joe as he stands quietly to one side. After everything that's been happening, it would be amazing for him if he won. Maybe it's just the confidence boost that he needs. And an extra three points wouldn't be that big a deal. Maybe Joe should have a bit more of an advantage anyway. I peer back down at the score sheet, lift my pen really casually, as if I'm just using it to count up the scores, and quickly change Joe's score to sixty-six.

"Joe, you're going to be the winner!" I tell him, my eyes wide and happy.

"No, he's not." A little girl with ginger plaits turns towards me. "Joe got sixty-three and I got sixty-five."

"Actually, Joe got sixty-six," I correct her.

"That's *cheating*!" The little girl's mouth drops open as

she tugs at the clipboard in my hand to have a look, her eyes growing wide as she sees the change on Joe's score. "You're *cheating*!"

"She made my score lower too." Alfie stomps over. "You're a big cheater. You just want Joe to win because he's short, like you!"

"I do not." I meet their eyes coolly. "I'm in charge of the skipping station and Joe's the winner. Well done, Joe!" I lift Joe's hand up to claim his win.

"I *didn't* win, Erin." Joe tugs his hand straight back down. "I came *third*. After Poppy and Otis." The little girl with the ginger plaits gives Joe a big smile. I guess she must be Poppy, but before I have a chance to say anything more about it, there's an announcement over the loudspeaker asking that all of the boys who participate in kung fu club make their way to the stage, where they will be giving a demonstration of their kung fu form.

"Joe," I gasp as I meet his eyes. "You don't have to do that. Maybe you should just stay here with me." I give him a reassuring pat on the arm. The absolute last thing Joe needs today is to get on a *stage*.

"Why not, Erin?" Joe shakes his head as I peer towards the stage, where a little group of children are gathering around Liam. "I'm in kung fu club. So, they mean *me*." He starts walking towards them.

"Really, Joe." I tug on his arm. "It's no big deal if you don't want to." But Joe just yanks his arm away and all I can do is watch, my heart in my mouth, as he completely ignores me and follows the little group of children on to the stage, taking a position right at the front.

He looks so small and alone as he stands next to Alfie and all of the other children that I don't think I can let him do this.

I take a deep breath, then I walk straight up on to the stage, and I stand next to him.

"Don't worry, Joe." I give all of the other boys on the stage my death stare. "I'm here with you."

"Erin!" Joe shakes his head. "You're making everyone *look*." He stares desperately out at the spectators. "Go *back, Erin*!" He hisses. "Go *back*." I hesitate as I stand on the stage beside Joe. Why doesn't he want my help? But as I look out at the crowd of children watching us, nudging each other and smiling that I'm up there with him, I realize what I've been doing.

I'm not being an Aimee for Joe. I'm being the *complete opposite*.

Aimee *never* got on a stage with me. Instead, she just

cheered me on and told me that I could do it. And Aimee would *never* let me win. She just helped me to properly *compete*. And if I couldn't compete fairly, she kept me company.

That's the difference between someone who sees *me* and someone who sees me as *less*.

I walk off the stage, everything becoming clear in my mind.

I've been pretending to Joe that even though we're shorter, everything is still the same for us.

And it's *not*.

It's harder.

And as I watch Joe demonstrate his kung fu form onstage, the only boy up there to get it perfectly right, I realize that it's time to stop promising to magically make things easier.

It's time to show Joe that he's enough exactly as he is. I need to be honest with him. I need to tell him that I shouldn't have made a promise that I might not be able to keep.

And suddenly, I *really* understand why Aimee wanted to use that first video. She wanted to show me that *I'm* enough, exactly as *I* am.

My stomach drops.

Aimee is quite possibly the best friend that I could *ever* have.

And I've lost her.

CHAPTER 29

Joe and I were both so tired after sports day that I didn't have a chance to talk to him about the whole promise thing, so when I wake up for school the next day, I decide that I'll talk to him after school today.

For the first time ever, Mum drives me to All Saints, because get this: apparently, Barbara and Pat aren't around until lunchtime because they went away for a night to Paris! I can't help smiling as I imagine Pat taking Barbara in a helicopter for dinner on the Eiffel Tower like he was dreaming of.

As I arrive at the school gates, Morgan meets me to carry my bag. She grins as soon as she sees me.

"I hear congratulations are in order?"

"Congratulations?" I frown, because I really don't know what she's talking about.

"Yes!" Morgan gives me a friendly nudge as if she can't believe that I've forgotten. "Your audition with Fusion Junior."

"*What?*" My jaw hits the floor. "What audition? Nobody told me!" I squeal in excitement as I grip her arm tightly, before marching towards the lift.

"I'm really sorry, I thought you'd know." Morgan jogs along behind me. "Isla and Sophia have been telling everyone all about it."

When I finally reach our form room, everyone is hanging around Isla and Sophia's desks, whispering *really* excitedly. I get on my tiptoes to try and see what's happening, even though that doesn't really make much difference, but my heart is starting to flutter in this nervous-excited way because I can see Isla is holding up her phone and I can hear my voice singing "Together" by Fusion. Is she seriously showing everyone in class the audition video before *me*? That doesn't seem right.

"Erin. . ." Aimee's hand reaches towards me as I make a beeline for Isla's desk, her eyes wide and worried. "Don't go over there."

"What?" I ask. "Why not?" I try to ignore that my heart has stopped fluttering and has started thudding very hard, because all of a sudden, something feels very, very wrong. Does Aimee know that I haven't seen the audition video yet? But before she has a chance to answer, I hear Grace say, "Wow! I cannot believe you've actually got an audition with *Fusion*! And *tonight*! That's incredible."

"We've got an audition?" I barge my way through to Isla and Sophia, and even though I'm feeling a little wrong-footed, this is majorly exciting. "Why didn't you tell me? I haven't even seen the video yet, let's see." I reach for Isla's phone as she pulls it away from my hand. "Can't I see it?" I laugh, then stop as I notice that nobody else is laughing. "Did you say the audition is *tonight*?" I plough on. "They didn't give us a lot of notice, did they?" I laugh again, then stop as Sophia meets my eyes and gives a little shake of her head.

"You *have* to tell her." She looks accusingly at Isla and everyone hushes around us.

"Tell me what?" My face falls and my stomach lurches because I am a hundred per cent certain that I am not going to like whatever it is that Sophia thinks Isla *has* to tell me. "What is it?"

Isla takes a really deep breath, then looks up towards the ceiling and says, "We knew about the audition on Monday. We didn't tell you because . . . well, because you're not in it."

"Not in it?" I must look really confused because I have no idea what she's talking about. "You mean that you got an audition, and I didn't?" My shoulders drop.

"No." Isla rolls her eyes as if I'm being really slow and annoying. "I mean that you're not *in* the audition video."

There's a gasp across the classroom and suddenly everyone gets really busy with something else. Anything to avoid watching this unfold.

Everyone except for Aimee, that is. She doesn't take her eyes off us.

"Of course I am." I shake my head and laugh. "I mean, I was *there*. I just heard my voice singing on your phone. How can I not be in the video?"

"We. . ." Isla looks at the floor. "We edited you out."

My heart starts to pound so loudly that I can hear it in my ears. I can't speak. I can barely breathe. All I can do is stand there looking like a prize lemon as my brain tries to catch up with Isla's words.

"You . . . *what*?" I finally manage.

"Look, I'm sorry." Isla shrugs. "You just . . . you stand out so much. We had to go with what worked, and I'm sorry, Erin, but you just didn't fit in enough, it looked ridiculous, so we had to edit you out. . ." She trails off.

"I stand out *too much*?" I repeat, because I have no idea how to put into words all of the things that are going through my mind right now. "But you've used my voice." I try to catch up. "I heard my voice when you were showing it to Grace."

"Yeah." Isla actually looks a bit shamefaced now. "For what it's worth, we didn't plan that. The producer just thought we sounded better with three voices." She looks at the floor. "Look, we never made any promises." She looks back up and meets my burning gaze. I almost laugh as I think of all the promises that *I've* been making. "I know you had your heart set on this." Her eyes soften. "Maybe you can come cheer us on and if we get into Fusion Junior, I could definitely introduce you to Shani, Robin and Brooke?"

I don't reply. I can't. I feel sick and my throat hurts and all I can think is that I feel an overwhelming need to sit down and *breathe*.

"Seats, please, everyone." Miss Wilson walks into the room and gives a sharp clap. She stops and looks from me to Isla, her eyes narrowing. "Is everything OK?" she asks.

"Yes, miss." Isla smiles sweetly.

"Erin?" Miss Wilson turns to me as Isla flashes me a nervous glance.

"Yes, miss." I nod, a huge lump in my throat. I walk to my desk, sit down, and try very hard to concentrate on my breathing.

CHAPTER 30

I'm not really sure what happens the rest of the afternoon.

I go to my lessons. I write stuff down.

Aimee keeps looking at me, but I don't look up.

She was totally and completely right about everything.

I don't have an audition.

I was wrong to work with Isla and Sophia.

I should never have made that promise to Joe.

But worst of all, now that all my hopes of getting into Fusion Junior are over, I've realized just how much I *wanted* it.

At the end of the day, I leave five minutes early to get my taxi, as usual, with Barbara carrying my bag as we head towards the school gates.

"Are you OK, Erin?" Barbara pulls open the door for me. "You're very quiet." I don't reply, just nod and keep looking at the floor. "I hear you got the audition with Fusion." She gives me a gentle pat on the arm as if she thinks I'm quiet because I'm nervous. "You must be pleased about that." I still don't reply. I'm guessing Barbara missed the memo about Isla and Sophia editing me out of our audition video, seeing as she wasn't in this morning, and I literally have no idea how to tell her. "When is it?" she asks.

"This afternoon, *apparently*," I answer as I look at my watch. "I expect Isla and Sophia will be leaving shortly."

"Oh." Barbara doesn't seem to understand. "Well, shouldn't you be meeting them, then?" Before I can answer, she starts walking up the corridor a lot faster, so I have to jog along behind her.

"No, Barbara, I—" I try to stop her as I follow her through the double doors into the playground, then stop talking as we both see Isla and Sophia ahead. They're getting into a car and looking all excited and for a second, I can't speak again. It's literally like a blow to the stomach.

"Girls!" Barbara seems to have the opposite reaction. While I stand there gawping, she starts trotting towards them. "Girls, wait for Erin!" Sophia's already in the car. Isla's just stepping in, but as she hears her name, she looks up and her whole face blanches. She probably thinks that

Barbara's about to give them a piece of her mind.

"Girls, wait! I'm sorry, I didn't realize!" Barbara turns back towards me, but I'm still not moving. In fact, I'm concentrating quite hard on breathing again. "Erin! Come *on*!" She hitches up her flowery dress and starts properly legging it towards Isla now. She's speedier than I'd have imagined, and I can't help remembering the whole bodyguard scenario.

Is Barbara going to actually body slam Isla to the ground?

But before she reaches them, Isla jumps into the car, shouts something very urgently to her mum, and they spin out of the car park.

Barbara stops. She leans over her legs to catch her breath, then looks up at me, completely confused. I think she's starting to realize that something has happened. But she can't think quickly enough to figure out what it is.

"Erin?" she asks, her face red and sweaty. "What's happened?"

"It doesn't matter." I march towards the gate.

"Erin?" She sighs, stands up and trots along after me.

"You're just here to carry my bag!" I round on her. "You don't need to know everything about me!" I watch her shrink back, as if I've slapped her round the face, and I immediately feel *so* bad. I know she's just trying to help, like I was trying to help Joe at sports day, but she's doing it *wrong* and the absolute *last* thing I need right now is her smothering me with attention. I don't want to explain what's happened. I don't even want to think about what's happened. I just want to go home. But how can I explain that to Barbara without, well, explaining? So, I just sigh and sit on the kerb as Barbara puts my bag down beside me without saying a word and quietly backs away through the school gates.

I'm not waiting long.

After a few minutes, Mum's car pulls up beside me, the passenger window opens and Dad's face smiles down at me.

"Hey, Erin!" He beams. I frown, because don't get me wrong, I'm really happy to see Mum and Dad, but why are they picking me up today? Did Barbara call them? Did they hear what happened? Are they here to take me for a McDonald's to cheer me up? But the first thing I say is, "Where's Joe?"

"Joe's at home with Nanny," Dad replies from out of the window. "We wanted to collect you today." He rubs Mum's tummy and gives me an excited wiggle of his eyebrows.

"Did you have a nice day, Erin?" Mum asks as I clamber into the car.

"Errr..." I don't really want to tell Mum and Dad about the audition video right now. And especially not before I've spoken to Joe. "It was fine." I shrug.

Mum and Dad share a look, before Dad turns around in his seat, peers at me closely, then turns back to Mum with a nod.

"Erin..." Mum gives her tummy another little rub. "We wanted to talk to you about the new baby." Dad turns back towards me and gives me a reassuring smile. "We had the twenty-week scan today," Mum continues, "and we found out that you're going to have a little baby sister."

"Oh!" I grin because even though I actually didn't mind about whether I was going to have a baby brother or sister, after the pants day that I've had, it's really nice to think about something else. "That's great news!" I pause as I remember that the twenty-week scan is also when Mum and Dad find out whether the baby has achondroplasia or not. And after the last few weeks of promises and worries, I've been thinking that even though I don't really mind, maybe it would be a good thing if the baby doesn't have it.

"And. . ." Mum reaches for Dad's hand. "Well, Erin," she continues, "she *doesn't have achondroplasia*." Mum's eyes meet mine in the rear-view mirror. "How do you feel about that?" she asks.

I don't say *anything*.

Because even though I was literally just thinking about how it might be a good thing if the baby doesn't have achondroplasia, when Mum said the words, it did not *feel* like a good thing.

In fact, as feelings go, it did not feel good at all . . . and I've already experienced some pretty bad feelings today.

"Erin?" Mum waits for me to say something. But I don't know what to say, because I don't want to tell Mum and Dad that as soon as Mum said that my baby sister does not have achondroplasia, the first image that sprang into my head was of Mum and Dad with their perfect little baby girl.

And it wasn't *me*.

I want to smile and say *oh, wow*, like I just did when Mum said that I'll be having a sister. But my stomach has clenched, and all of these horrible images have dived straight into my brain.

Dad and my baby sister going on a roller coaster together, while I stand watching them to one side, too short to be allowed on it.

Mum taking my baby sister shopping for clothes that fit her *perfectly* from *any* shop.

My baby sister on the stage, best friends with Isla Walsh, singing with Fusion.

"That's ... *great*." I finally manage a watery smile, before I concentrate really hard on looking out of the window, because I really don't want to feel like this, but I don't know how to switch off all the thoughts that I'm having right now.

My baby sister reaching a toilet door handle without using a shoe.

My baby sister being seen at a make-up counter.

My baby sister walking into a room without being stared at.

"Erin?" Dad turns back to peer at me again as he reaches his hand towards me. "However you're feeling, that's OK. You can talk to us about it, you know?"

"I'm really sorry." I try really hard not to cry, but however much I blink, I can't stop the tears from rolling down my face. "I just..." I swallow hard. I'm getting this all wrong. I don't want Mum and Dad to think I'm unhappy about the baby, because I'm not. I'm really excited to have a baby sister, whether she has achondroplasia or not. "It hasn't been a very good day," I finally blurt out.

"Why? What's happened at school today?" Mum asks, her voice full of concern now. Her unspoken problem alarm must be clanging pretty hard. I can see her mind whirring into overdrive as she imagines all the things that might have happened to me today. Finally, I see her face clear.

"The audition," she recalls. "You heard back?" She doesn't wait for me to answer. Just assumes that I've heard and that I didn't get a callback. "Don't worry, Erin. Everyone gets rejections. You mustn't think—"

"I didn't make it on to the audition *video*." I swipe a tear from my cheek as I finally say the awful words out loud. "Isla used my voice, but she had me edited out. She said I stood out too much. She said it looked ridiculous." I try to swallow down my sob, but I just can't. My throat feels thick and I feel so tired, like my whole body is flooding with this heavy sadness that it can't hold in for one second longer.

I hear Mum and Dad's intake of breath and that's it. I lose it. The gasping, wrenching sobs take over as my whole body convulses with them. My mouth feels gummy with saliva and my back hurts, but I just can't stop it now. Not when Dad undoes his seat belt and climbs over the passenger seat to hug me and not when Mum stops the car and runs desperately into the back seat to hold me.

"I'm so sorry, Erin," I hear them soothe as I lean in towards them.

CHAPTER 31

"How are you feeling, pet?" Nanny opens the front door to welcome us home as Joe smiles out from behind her legs. She hesitates as she sees my red eyes. "Oh, Erin." She throws her arms around me as Mum and Dad shuffle in behind me. "Are you OK, love?" She stands back, both hands on my shoulders as she checks me over.

"Yeah." I wriggle out of her arms, then lean down to give Joe a hug.

I've spent the last three weeks trying to avoid this exact moment, and suddenly I don't think that I can avoid it for one *second* longer.

"Joe, I'm really sorry but I should never have promised you that I could get into Fusion Junior." I swallow down another sob as I shake my head.

"Did you not get in?" he asks, his eyes wide and serious.

"No, Joe." I blink hard as I try not to start crying again. "I didn't get in."

Joe doesn't say anything right away, and for a second I'm so scared that he's going to stop talking again, like the last time I broke a promise to him.

"It's OK, Erin." He hugs my leg hard.

"You mean you're not upset with me?" I hug him back. "That I didn't keep my promise to you?"

Joe stands back and shakes his head.

"You tried your best, Erin." He shrugs, then leans forward to whisper in my ear. "We can be anything. Just not everyone knows it yet."

"Oh, Joe." I squeeze him tight. "You're so smart." I cannot believe how much I've underestimated Joe recently. I've been so stupid to get so worked up about this promise.

"You both are." Nanny tilts her head to one side. "Now, I've made spaghetti bolognese. Why don't you go and get changed and then we can have a nice chinwag about things?"

"Thanks, Nanny, but I'm not really hungry." I try to ignore the look on Nanny's face when I say that, because now she knows that this is *serious*.

I *never* refuse Nanny's spaghetti bolognese.

I put my head down, walk up to my room, close the door behind me and flop on to my bed.

I wish I could chat to Aimee. She'd know exactly what to say to make me feel better. I try to picture her standing here and think about what she'd say right now. I sigh. If I'd just stuck with Aimee in the first place, I wouldn't need to be picturing her; she'd be here. In fact, none of this would have even happened. We'd probably just be sitting here listening to music and chatting.

There's a knock on the door. I don't answer.

"Should we just go in?" I hear Nanny's muffled whisper outside.

"I think so," Mum answers her.

The door opens slowly, and Mum and Nanny walk cautiously into my room, like two nervous gamekeepers walking into a lion's den. Nanny's carrying a tray of spaghetti bolognese; Mum's holding the biscuit tin aloft.

They stop and look at me flopped on my bed, then sigh and put the tray of spaghetti bolognese and the biscuit tin on my desk.

"Your mum's filled me in on what happened today, love." Nanny sits down beside me. "That Isla's got a lot to answer for." I shrug and move to one side to make room for them and they both sit on the edge of the bed.

"Do you want to talk about it?" Mum asks.

"Not really." I shake my head.

Mum and Nanny never make me talk if I don't want to. So, we just sit in silence, and it actually feels kind of nice.

Nanny picks up my bag from the weekend, pulls out my denim jacket, and looks at it for a few seconds. She searches inside the bag for *The Jam* letters and pulls them out too, then takes out a needle and thread from her handbag and starts sewing them back on.

My tummy rumbles and I sit up as Mum gets down from my bed and passes me the tray of spaghetti bolognese. I eat a forkful. It's so delicious. Nanny makes the best spaghetti bolognese ever. I take another bite. Mum and Nanny sit quietly beside me. Eventually, after my third mouthful, Mum doesn't seem able to stay quiet any longer.

"I know it's hard sometimes, Erin." She pats my hand gently. "I've been where you are."

I turn towards Mum. She always seems so tough and strong and so comfortable with herself. Has she *really* been here?

"There's always an Isla." Mum smiles sadly. "And you can only be you."

"You have to run your own race, Erin." Nanny looks up from her sewing. My face must show that I don't really know what she's talking about, so she carries on. "If you like singing, then you should sing. If you like dancing, then you should dance. You just have to do what makes *you* happy. It doesn't matter what anyone else thinks."

"What about when I don't feel like being me?" I ask. "What about when I don't know what will make me happy?"

"Family." Mum holds my hand. "They get you through most things." She looks at the photo of me and Aimee on the desk. "Friends too." She gives my hand a squeeze. "Real friends, anyway."

I follow her gaze to the photo. I need to make things right with Aimee.

Then I remember Barbara's face at the school gates earlier. "I think I upset Barbara," I say. "She tries so hard to help me. It just feels like too much sometimes."

"Maybe you just need to teach her, Erin?" Mum puts her head to one side and sidles up towards me. "Maybe we just need to teach everyone."

We meet each other's gaze, and we smile, like we're having this quiet moment of smiley understanding.

"I hear that Erin's stopped eating!" Dad marches into the room like the house is on fire, a huge bar of chocolate held aloft, Joe giggling from his shoulders.

He stops as he sees the half-eaten plate of spaghetti bolognese on my lap.

"Oh, good." He breathes a sigh of relief. "Crisis averted. But just to be on the safe side. . ." He rips open the chocolate bar and winks at me. "I think we need to make a start on this."

CHAPTER 32

The next day at school, I feel really nervous.

I need to make things right with Aimee somehow.

But first I need to make things right with Barbara. I sit in Pat's taxi watching the clock as we drive slowly to school, preparing a little speech in my head ready for when she meets me at the school gates this morning.

But as Pat drives carefully into the school gates, it's not Barbara who's waiting there for me. It's Aimee. I know I've been thinking about how much I want to make it up with Aimee and how much I've got everything wrong, but as soon as I see her, my heart picks up speed and I get this nervous flutter, because I'm not sure what's going to happen next.

"Hi, Erin," she says as soon as I'm out of the car.

"Barbara said that I could carry your bag this morning instead of her." She holds her hand out to take my bag.

"Oh, OK." I pass over my bag, even though I feel a bit weird and awkward about it. "Errr, thanks." I smile and I look at the ground, because I have not prepared a speech for Aimee yet and I don't think I can use the same one that I was going to use for Barbara.

We start walking towards class, neither of us saying anything. But as we're waiting for the lift, Aimee turns towards me.

"I'm really sorry, Erin." She shuffles her feet. "I should never have said that you don't believe in yourself. I wasn't a very good friend."

"Aimee, you're an *amazing* friend!" I exclaim. I can't believe that Aimee would think she's been a bad friend, when all she's ever been is brilliant. And just like that, all of the weird tension between us disappears like a cloud of smoke. "I'm so sorry I didn't see that before." I meet her eyes as the lift doors open and we step inside.

The atmosphere rises as quickly as the lift as we smile at each other, and it's like it's just me and Aims again.

Jam and cheese.

"You were right, though." Aimee gives me a friendly

nudge. "I should have supported you a bit more with the Fusion Junior video. I let myself get all offended after Isla said that it wasn't professional enough, even though I knew that you just wanted to give yourself the best possible chance. But then when you started making new friends in class ... well..." She looks at the floor. "I guess I got jealous and stayed away. I'm really sorry. I wanted to talk to you that day in PE, but then I saw you were working on the audition video with Isla and Sophia, and I guess I just thought maybe they'd be better friends than me."

"Ha!" I can't help snorting. "Honestly, Aims, they have been the worst friends *EVER*."

"Yeah." Aimee shakes her head. "I *noticed*. So..." She leans in towards me as the lift doors open and we step out. "How's Joe? Have you talked to him about ... you know, your promise?"

"Yeah." I nod. "He was amazing, Aims. He took it really well." I feel this lovely warm glow as Aimee throws her arms around me and hugs me really tight. I cannot believe that I let a super-long-shot audition video get in the way of our friendship.

"So..." Aimee asks, "how are you feeling about the whole audition thing now? I mean, I know it hasn't exactly worked out, but did it feel good to get back into singing?"

"Yeah." My whole body feels lighter as I remember what it felt like to perform. "It felt great, Aims. I know that my chances were slim, and I know that I wanted it to keep my promise to Joe, but actually when I was singing and dancing, I loved it so much. My nan said something to me last night that got me thinking that maybe being edited out of Isla and Sophia's audition video was for the best after all. It was something about running my own race, which might sound weird, but when I had the makeover with Isla and Sophia, something felt all wrong, like I was in the wrong lane. Like I was trying to be someone *else*. Like you said all along." I glance up sheepishly. "I just didn't listen." Aimee smiles sadly. "I've been thinking about joining a drama club or asking Mum about getting some singing lessons. I think I'd like to keep going with the performing."

"That's great, Erin."

"Yeah," I agree. "I just wish I'd listened to you in the first place, Aims. You were right the *whole time*. I wish so badly that we'd just sent the first video, the one you edited. It was *so* good! I can't believe I let Isla get in my head." I roll my eyes.

"Erin?" Aimee pulls her phone out, the corners of her mouth twitching. "I'm really glad you've said that because actually. . ." She pauses. "I submitted the video anyway."

CHAPTER 33

"You *what*?" I grab her arm as we stand there outside the lift in the corridor leading to our form room.

"Yep." Aimee beams. "I just loved it so much. And I really do believe you could win it, Erin. I didn't know how else to show you. I wanted to tell you about it, but you seemed so busy working with Isla and Sophia and I wasn't sure if you'd be happy about it."

"Aims, you are the *best*!" I throw my arms around her, because this is *properly amazing*.

Ever since I got cut from Isla and Sophia's audition tape, I've been wishing and wondering. And now it turns out that Aimee actually submitted the video!

Wait. Does that mean I might actually have a chance of getting an audition for Fusion Junior?

"There's just one problem." Aimee seems to read

my mind. "I've been keeping an eye on my emails, you know, just in case you got an audition and I haven't seen anything . . . not *yet* anyway." She gives me a playful nudge. "So, I double-checked Fusion's website and it says that all successful applicants will be informed by the end of today." She pulls out her phone with a cheeky wiggle of her eyebrows. "And I haven't looked since last night."

"OMG, Aimee!" I squeal. "Check your emails *now*!"

My heart is hammering so hard as we scroll through Aimee's emails. When we don't see any from today, Aimee continues scrolling back further, just to be sure. She has a lot of emails from her bank (OMG, Aimee's dog-walking has made her rich!), some requests for dog-walking and a subscription to a fashion magazine.

But there are no emails from Fusion.

I do not have an audition.

"Oh, Erin, I'm so sorry." Aimee shoves her phone in her pocket. "I really thought you might have a chance."

"It's OK." My shoulders relax as Joe's words come back to me, the ones where he said that we can be anything, but that maybe not everyone knows it yet, and I realize that I actually feel OK!

"You know it doesn't mean anything, right?" Aimee is clearly trying to make me feel better.

"I'm OK, Aims." I smile, and I mean it because I really am. "It was always a long shot. I'm just glad that Fusion actually saw my video. That's pretty cool, isn't it?"

"It's super cool." Aimee nudges me as I notice a poster on the corridor noticeboard.

All Saints All Girls
Christmas Play

AUDITIONS

Can you sing? Can you dance?
Then we want to see you!

Auditions will be held on
4 November at lunchtime
in the drama studio.

All welcome.

I turn to Aimee, my smile wide. After all I've been through these past few weeks, I think I am ready to try to perform in front of a massive live audience again.

"Erin!" Aimee jumps up and down in excitement. "You should do it!"

We walk into form class together chatty and happy. It

feels so good to have Aimee back.

"Hey, Erin." Morgan beams as I take my seat. I can't help noticing that my stool and cushions are all ready and waiting for me, even though Barbara is nowhere in sight. "See you at basketball practice later, right?"

"Definitely." I smile, because even though I mostly joined the team to help at Joe's sports day, I'm so happy that I made it on to the squad.

"Great!" Morgan gives me a thumbs up, but then we all stop and look up as Isla and Sophia walk into the room, their heads down, their faces pink.

"I expect you're happy now." Isla glares at me, then walks to her desk. What's she on about?

"What happened?" Morgan asks as I shrug in reply.

"Karma happened." Aimee leans over with a sage nod. "I didn't just email Fusion your audition video. I also emailed them yesterday to tell them that Isla and Sophia had used your voice on their video without your permission."

"No way!" My mouth falls open.

"Too right." Aimee crosses her arms. "No one treats *my* best friend like that."

"Sophia told me about it on the bus this morning," Grace whispers as she leans over from her desk.

"Apparently Fusion were *really* unimpressed. Isla and Sophia's audition was cancelled as soon as they arrived."

"Wow." I peer over my shoulder to Isla and Sophia. They don't look back up.

"What goes around, comes around." Morgan raises her eyebrows. "As far as I'm concerned, that's the least they deserve."

The rest of the day actually goes really well. Aimee and I are like cheese and jam all over again. We laugh, and giggle, and she even comes to watch my basketball practice.

I hardly see Barbara all day.

She keeps out of sight and just makes sure that my bag, cushion and stool are in the right place for each lesson, keeping in the background. She's obviously avoiding me and I feel so bad. I really need to apologize to her.

I get my chance at the end of the day, when Barbara silently walks me to the school gates.

"Barbara." I start with the speech I prepared in Pat's taxi this morning. "I'm really sorry about yesterday. I'd—"

"Oh, Erin," Barbara interrupts. "You don't need to be sorry about *anything*. I'm the one who should be sorry." She shakes her head. "Pat kept telling me that I was being a bit overenthusiastic, but I just wouldn't listen."

"I . . . um. . ." Barbara's kind of interrupted my apology and now I can't remember the little speech that I'd prepared, so I just say, "Are you and Pat, like, a proper couple now, then?"

"Yes." Barbara goes all fluttery. "I think he might be . . . the one."

"Oh, that's great!" I beam, all thoughts of speeches forgotten. Pat and Barbara seem to suit each other so well and this whole lovey-dovey vibe is super-sweet.

"Anyway, Erin," Barbara continues, "I called your old class helper, Liam, last night and he's given me a few tips." She pulls out a notebook full of handwritten notes. "And if there's anything I'm doing that is unhelpful or, well. . ." She falters, takes a deep breath and rushes on: ". . . *too much* . . . then I want you to know that you can tell me."

"OK, then," I agree, because Aimee was right: Barbara's nice, really. And maybe Mum was right, too: maybe Barbara just needs me to guide her a bit sometimes.

"We'll be grand." Barbara opens her arms wide to hug me.

"Ummm." I hesitate.

"Oh, of course." Barbara's neck flushes a little pink. "Bear with me." Her arms drop. "It's a work in progress."

And that's when I throw my arms around her.

"Oh, Erin!" She hugs me back. "Thank you."

As we arrive at the gates, I'm super happy to see that Dad's waiting to collect me. I think he must've been worried about me after last night. I hope he's brought more chocolate with him.

"Hey, Dad." I give him a friendly wave, then climb into the car.

"All OK today, Erin?" Dad turns back to look at me, his eyes never leaving my face as he waits for me to answer.

"Yep." I smile and I really mean it. "Is it OK if we wait for Aimee? Then we can give her a lift too."

"Absolutely." Dad's face lights up. "That would be class."

The rest of the evening, Aimee and I don't stop chatting. She laughs so much when I tell her about the receptionist at Glow You and she giggles when I tell her about Joe's sports day, especially when I tell her that I halved Alfie's score. It feels so good to have my best friend back.

But when she heads home later and I wave her goodbye from my window, I can't help wondering if I ever really had a hope of getting into Fusion Junior.

I drop down from my bed and pick up the photo of me and Joe.

If I ever really had a hope of keeping my promise to Joe.

Because if Isla and Sophia got an audition using my voice, then why didn't *I* get an audition using *my* voice?

I sigh and sit on the edge of the bed as I think back to the time that I froze onstage. That first time in primary school when Isla sang instead of me. I remember standing there in the middle of the stage, Isla's words ringing in my ears about how everyone would love me no matter how I sang, wondering if that meant that I didn't really *deserve* to be there.

I put the photo back down and flop back on to my bed as I turn to look at the Fusion poster.

Will I ever really be picked to be in a show just because I'm good enough?

Can people see *past* my size?

I see the half-eaten chocolate bar from last night on my desk, sit up and break off a chunk. I don't really know the answer to my questions, but chocolate will help me feel better for now.

CHAPTER 34

The next morning, I wake up to the sound of a car horn outside our house.

I pull the pillow over my head, because seriously? It's, like, 6 a.m. or something!

Beeeeeeep.

The car horn blares again.

Beeeeeeeeeeeepppppppppp.

"What on earth is going on?" Dad wanders into my room, his hair ruffled, his pyjama's crumpled, his face like thunder.

Beeeeeeeeeeeepppppppppp.

He opens the window, takes a deep breath, and yells "OI!", ready to hurl abuse at the prize idiot parked outside our house, and—

"Aimee?" he calls down. "What are *you* doing here?"

"Aimee?" I ask from under my pillow. "Are you sure?"

"Yep," Dad replies. "She's in Pat's taxi with Pat and Barbara."

"*What?*" I throw the pillow off and stand on my bed to join Dad at the window as Aimee waves her phone over her head.

"Check your phone!" She points to it; then puts it to her ear, as if we're playing an elaborate game of charades. I duck my head back inside and pick up my phone from my bedside table.

OMG, I have sixty-three missed calls from Aimee and seven messages!

5.33 a.m.
Erin! Just woke up with a thought. . . what if
the email from Fusion went into my junk???
YOU HAVE AN AUDITION!!!!!!!!!!

5.36 a.m.
I just called them to explain and they actually
answered!!! Erin, I was freaking out! They're
on their way to the airport. I explained it all
and THEY STILL WANT TO SEE YOU!!!!!!!!!!

5.37 a.m.

They're boarding a flight to LA at 7.15 this morning! YOU HAVE TO GET TO THE AIRPORT NOW!!!!!!!!!!!! Btw I'm calling your mum so she can drive us there.

5.38 a.m.

Rise and shine, Erin! You have an audition with Fusion! And can you wake up your mum too? She's not answering!

5.38 a.m.

Seriously, Erin, this is no time to be asleep. WAKE UP!!!!!!!!!!!

5.40 a.m.

Right. Seeing as you and your mum won't answer, I've called Pat. He's on his way. I'm not going to let you miss this audition, Erin!

5.41 a.m.

SERIOUSLY, ERIN, WAKE UP!!!!!!!!!!

5.42 a.m.

WAAAAAAAAAAKKKKKKKKKKE
UUUUUUUPPPPPPPPPPPP!!!!!!!!!!!!!!!

OMG!

I dive back to the window as Aimee meets my eyes with the biggest, happiest grin.

"I knew it, Erin! I knew they'd want to see you! Come on! We have to get to the airport, right *now*! We don't have long to get there!"

"What's going on?" Mum walks into the room, tying her dressing gown cord into place. "Why do I have eighty-three missed calls from Aimee? What's she shouting for outside our house? And why's Pat here?" She peers out of the window. "And Barbara? It's not even a school day!" She huffs. "I think we might need to talk to that woman about *boundaries*."

"I've got an *audition*!" I nearly scream at Mum. "Fusion want to see me! But they're flying to LA this morning. Aimee says we have to get to the airport right now, before their flight leaves. We've got an hour."

"*Whaaaat?* One hour to get to the airport?" Mum does not look convinced that that's a possibility.

"Yeah." My shoulders drop and I shake my head as I

look at my watch. "You're right. It's too late. We'll never make it in time. Of course I can't go to the airport for an audition with Fusion. What am I thinking? I don't even have a routine."

"*WHAT?*" Mum marches to my wardrobe, opens it and throws my black leggings, vest and denim jacket at me. "You have been trying to get this audition for weeks, Erin. You can't give up now! Now get dressed and get your *be-hind* in that taxi." She marches out, then stops and turns back to Dad, who's still standing at the window, watching proceedings with a bemused smile on his face. "Come on!" She claps her hands as Dad stops smiling and stands to attention. "Our daughter is not going to the biggest audition of her life without us. We're all going." She marches back to the window and shouts down to Pat. "We'll need to pick up Erin's nan on the way!"

"Shouldn't we just drive ourselves there?" Dad asks. "We can pick her up on the way and meet Erin at the airport?"

"Not a chance." Mum shakes her head. "What if they get there first? Nope, this family is sticking together."

Ten minutes later and me, Aimee, Mum, Dad, Joe, Nanny and Barbara are all crammed into Pat's taxi. We're all fired up and Mum's looking seriously frenzied.

"Go! Go! Go!" She drums the seat.

Mum has clearly never been in a car with Pat before.

His head turns towards her as he explains that he is a safe driver and she needn't worry. Then he inspects that we're all wearing our seat belts, before checking his mirrors, indicating, and pulling away at a snail's pace.

It kills the vibe, just a little bit.

"Slow and steady wins the race." He tells us all over his shoulder, his eyes never leaving the road.

"Errrrr. We'll get to the airport on time, will we?" Mum looks at her watch, then peers longingly out of the back window towards our car.

"Oh, sure we will." Pat raises his eyebrows confidently as he looks at the dashboard clock. "We'll be there at 6.48 a.m."

"Well, that's very precise, that is." Dad looks impressed as we all relax, just a little bit.

"They've said that they'll meet you at the Causeway Lounge at 6.50 a.m." Aimee scrolls through her phone. "Do you think that's a bit tight? Two minutes?"

Everyone meets each other's eyes with a hopeful shrug.

"Isn't the Causeway Lounge after security?" Nanny asks. "How are we supposed to get to it?"

Aimee checks her phone again.

"They've said that someone should be there to meet us." She looks up.

"Aimee?" I grab her arm. "What if I can't sing in front of them? What if I freeze?" I sit back in my seat, my heart pumping hard. "I don't even have a dance routine." I look up at Aimee, feeling completely panicked. "Do we have any music?"

"Don't worry, Erin." Aimee meets my eyes. "Just do what you did when we made the video. Pretend that nobody's watching you. You didn't have a routine when we made the video either, remember? You can freestyle, like you did before. And as for the music . . ." She holds up her phone. ". . . we'll use the same songs as before. Just trust me, OK?"

Does Aimee seriously think that I can pretend that nobody is watching me while standing in front of Fusion, the greatest girl band on earth? And as for freestyling, is that *really* going to be good enough? Because it doesn't feel like it. Aimee must be able to see what I'm thinking. She leans forward, puts her hand on my arm and smiles reassuringly.

"I believe in you, Erin. Your natural talent will shine through. I promise."

We meet each other's eyes as I nod and it's this really special moment. That is, until we hear a snort from beside us as Mum, Dad and Nanny fall about giggling.

"Aimee Dowling!" Mum gives Aimee a playful nudge. "Honestly, I've never heard anything so *cheesy*! Is that why you're called 'The Cheese'?"

"But seriously" – Dad wipes a tear from his eye – "you're not really going to just *freestyle*?"

"Well, yeah!" I try to look more confident than I feel. "I don't exactly have a choice."

"Oh." Dad sits up now. "You were serious."

"It won't matter much if we don't move a bit faster," Mum mutters as the taxi ambles along towards a traffic light ahead of us. It turns orange, then red, and Pat brings us to a steady stop.

"There are, err, quite a few traffic lights on this road, Pat." Dad leans forward as we all look out of the driver's window at the road ahead, which is basically a line of traffic lights all the way to the airport. "I don't like to tell you how to drive, Pat, but you might want to put your foot down next time." He sits back and wiggles his eyebrows confidently to let us know that the situation is handled.

"Don't you worry," Pat reassures us as the traffic light

turns green and we pull slowly away. "I know what I'm doing."

The taxi drives steadily on towards the next traffic light ahead, our eyes never leaving it as we all hold our breath in hope that it will remain green.

It doesn't.

It turns orange, then red, and Pat brings us once again to a slow and steady stop.

"You didn't want to put your foot down there, then, Pat?" Dad speaks through gritted teeth.

"I'm grand, thanks," Pat replies tightly.

For the next five traffic lights, every one of them turns red as we reach them, Pat bringing us to a slow and steady stop, Dad getting more and more frustrated with every passing moment.

We all look at the clock as it turns 6.47 a.m.

"Well, I guess we won't be there for 6.48 a.m. after all." Dad flops back into his seat and glares at Pat as we reach yet another red light, one more traffic light still between us and the airport.

"Oh." Pat looks at the clock, his eyes darting towards Barbara in the seat next to him. "Well, I really don't want you to be late." He taps the steering wheel agitatedly, clearly wrestling with himself as he stares at the traffic lights ahead. "Maybe, if we just go a little bit. . ." He raises one hand towards his mouth, his fist clenched as he strains to say the word. "A little bit. . ." His fist begins tapping his mouth.

"Pat, are you biting your fist?" Dad sits forward again as Pat's eyes begin to water.

"Faster." Pat finally pushes the word out. Panting, he unclenches his fist and revs the engine.

The traffic light turns orange, then turns green, and we're all thrown back as Pat slams his foot on the accelerator. We all scramble forwards, our faces pushed back by the G-force of speed as the taxi flies towards it like a bullet, our eyes never leaving that last traffic light ahead.

It turns orange.

Pat doesn't stop.

It turns red.

Pat still doesn't stop and we fly into the drop-off point at the airport with a screech of brakes.

"There we are." Pat pulls out a hankie and mops his brow as he points to the clock just as it turns to 6.48 a.m. "Told you." He turns towards us all, his smile wide. "Good luck, Erin."

CHAPTER 35

We all pile out of the car and leg it into the airport, and we don't even care that everyone is stopping to look at us, because Fusion are waiting and I am *not* going to miss this audition!

I look at the clock just as it turns to 6.50 a.m. I'm supposed to be meeting Fusion in the Causeway Lounge *right now*.

"Where's this person who's meeting us?" Mum asks as Aimee starts desperately scrolling through her phone. "Will they still be waiting?"

"I'm not sure." She looks up as we all crowd around her, desperately searching for anyone who could be meeting us.

"Never mind." Mum takes charge. "Let's just get straight to this Causeway Lounge." She scans the airport, then marches up to a lady at a baggage desk. "Excuse me, where's the Causeway Lounge? My daughter has an audition with Fusion. Someone was supposed to be meeting her?"

"Where are you flying to?" the lady asks wearily.

"Oh, we're not flying." Mum shakes her head. "My daughter has—"

"Then you're not going into the lounge," the lady interrupts her. "It's the other side of security."

"Don't worry!" Dad pulls out his wallet. "I know *exactly* what to do. I've seen this before in an episode of *Friends*. How much for a ticket?"

"Errr..." The lady gives Dad a long look. "It doesn't work like that. You can't buy tickets at the airport any more."

"Don't you worry, Erin." Dad whips his phone out. "There's bound to be an easyJet flight I can buy for twenty quid!" But as he scrolls through his phone, I notice the clock above the baggage desk just as it turns to 6.53 a.m.

We're late.

We all stop and look at each other, because how on earth are we going to get to the lounge now? We've obviously missed the person who was supposed to meet us. We can't get past security. We don't have a ticket. And actually, we're late now too.

If this were a movie, then at this moment, I'd run and jump over the barriers and leg it into the Causeway Lounge, trailed by six security guards.

Except this isn't a movie and I'm three foot five. I'm not going to be jumping over any barriers.

Aimee taps the redial button and calls Fusion's people.

"Hi," she says breathlessly. "Erin Woods is here for her audition. I think somebody was supposed to be here to meet us. Oh." She stops. "It was you? Did you wait until—" She stops again as someone on the other end of the line continues talking. "Yes." Aimee nods. "She's here. But we can't get past security. Is there any way that—" She pauses as the person on the other end speaks again. "But we're *here*." She sounds a little desperate. "Have they boarded yet, because surely—"

We all hear the tannoy overhead and my stomach drops. "Flight LAX9116. Last call for boarding."

Are we *really* too late? Have I *really* missed my chance?

I look out through the window leading out to the runway and, OMG, I actually *see* Shani, Robin and Brooke walking across the tarmac towards the plane! They're wearing trackie bottoms and hoodies, but I would recognize them *anywhere*. There's a small woman trotting along beside them on the phone. That must be who Aimee's talking to. I tug on Aimee's jacket and point out of the window excitedly, because *that's actually Fusion down there!*

"We can see you!" Aimee starts tapping on the window as she speaks into the phone. "Look. We're right here!"

We both start *really* waving as the lady turns and looks directly at us. She gives a hesitant wave, then shakes her head and talks back into the phone.

"But you're *right there*. And we're *right here!*" Aimee's waving out of the window pretty desperately now. "Can't you just ask Shani, Robin or Brooke? I bet they'd say—"

The lady glances up at Shani, Robin and Brooke, then shakes her head again and continues talking on the phone.

And then Aimee does something that is very *un-Aimee*. "Look!" She sounds properly *firm*. "You asked us to come here this morning so that my friend could audition for Fusion, and. . ." She hesitates as the lady interrupts and I watch as she hurries along the tarmac behind Fusion speaking animatedly into the phone. Aimee ignores her and takes a deep breath as she pulls the phone away from her ear. "Oh my god, look!" She calls over her shoulder really loudly. "It's Fusion!" And she starts pointing out of the window as a group of excited fans gather next to us, before whispering into the phone. "There are loads of people here, and I'm guessing you don't want us all to start posting our disappointment on social media about coming all the way down to the airport *on time* for an audition with Fusion, do you?"

There's a long pause.

From out of the window, the lady gives us another look, then taps Shani on the arm, says something and points towards us as the crowd of fans all wave excitedly towards them.

Shani stops, looks up and waves to the fans as I watch, my eyes wide and hopeful.

"I'm on hold," Aimee whispers, putting the phone on loudspeaker so that I can hear what happens next and we watch and listen as Shani, Robin and Brooke all stop and have a bit of a confab. There's a lot of nodding and head shaking and turning to look in our direction, and then a voice comes out of the phone: "Tell your friend she has two minutes. We're coming to you. Be ready."

And the next thing I know, Shani, Robin and Brooke pull their hoods over their heads and start walking towards us.

CHAPTER 36

"Just don't start until I tell you!" Aimee grips my arm tightly, then legs it, and I watch as she literally *sprints* across the airport.

"Where's *she* going?" Nanny asks.

"I don't know." I shake my head as I watch her go, feeling completely out of my depth. "But Fusion are coming here to see me right now."

"*Here?*" Dad asks as he joins the family huddle.

"Yes." I nod.

"In front of all these people?" Mum asks as she grips Nanny's hand.

"Yes." I nod again.

"So, why is Aimee legging it over *there?*" Dad points towards Aimee as she pelts it down a corridor, signposted Baggage Claim and Information Desk.

"Maybe she needs the toilet?" Barbara suggests as we watch her run until she's out of sight.

"She must need the toilet really badly," Dad comments.

"I guess." I shake my head. I wish Aimee had told me what she was planning. Fusion are headed here right now and whatever it is, I can't help thinking it would be easier if she had stayed here. "But she's got the backing track for my song, and she's got the music for my dance."

"Oh." Mum, Dad, Nanny and Barbara all share a look.

"Could you sing without a backing track?" Mum suggests hopefully. "I mean, if you had to."

"I guess." I shrug. "But what am I supposed to *dance* to without any music?"

"Oh, Erin. This is a pickle, to be sure." Nanny shakes her head.

"I could sing?" Barbara joins the huddle. "Could you dance to that? I often get compliments for my rendition of 'Whiskey in the Jar'. I do love an Irish ballad."

Mum, Dad, and Nanny blink at her for a moment, before Dad turns towards me.

"Do you think you could you dance to 'Whiskey in the Jar', Erin?" he asks.

"What about a Fusion song?" Nanny asks Barbara. "Do you know any of them?"

But before we have a chance to talk about it any more, Fusion, the greatest girl band on earth, walk out of the doors and head directly towards me.

I watch, hardly daring to breathe as they all walk towards me, smiling and waving at the crowd staring at them ... just like *I* do, when people stare at me.

They look kind of different to when I watched them in concert. They're just wearing ordinary clothes and they've got no make-up on, and they're *way* smaller than I thought, and I can't help thinking that they're actually just real people, like me.

Maybe this doesn't have to be as scary as I thought.

"Hey, girl." Shani bends down to speak to me, her massive Afro peeking out from inside her hood. "So, you want to audition for us today?"

I nod, my heart beating so hard, barely trusting myself to speak, let alone sing.

"All right." Her eyes soften. "I'm sorry you have to do this here. But we'd love to hear you sing 'Together'. Can you do it?"

I nod again as Shani stands back up and I realize that this is my moment.

I *cannot* blow it.

*

I'm standing in the airport in front of Shani, Robin and Brooke as they wait politely for me to sing for them.

I swallow hard.

This feels, well . . . *big*.

And I'm blowing it.

I'd feel pretty uncomfortable singing in front of *any*one in the airport at *any* time, but this feels way worse.

I have no backing track. Nothing. Just me, my voice, an enormous airport, and *Fusion* . . . oh, and loads of their fans!

I turn to Mum, Dad, Nanny and Barbara as they stand to one side, nudging each other and shuffling their feet as if someone should *do* something to help me, but nobody knows what to do.

Joe peeks out at me from behind Mum's legs.

I glance in the direction that Aimee ran off to. What was she on about when she said not to start until she *tells me*? Because she's not even *here*.

And now I don't know *what* to do.

I blink, turn back to Shani, Robin and Brooke and I try to plaster a reassuring smile on my face, because I have to do *something*.

A bead of sweat trickles down my back.

I was so determined to sing for them a minute ago,

but now it suddenly seems like this could quite possibly be the very worst moment of my *whole life*.

I take a deep breath and open my mouth to sing . . . then close it again.

The lady who was on the phone to Aimee sighs and looks at her watch as Shani gives me this encouraging nod, like she's persuading a newborn lamb to take its first steps.

"Why are we all standing here watching this poor kid?" I hear a passer-by turn towards someone next to him.

"Ooh, look, there's a whole family of them!" I hear someone else say.

I turn to Mum, Dad, Nanny, Joe and Barbara as they all stand there, ignoring all of the onlookers, gripping each other's hands tightly. Hardly daring to blink.

"I'm so sorry." I shake my head. "I don't think. . ." I stop as I feel a small hand take mine and I look down to see *Joe*.

"Show them, Erin," he whispers as he pulls me down towards him. "Show them we can be *anything*."

I grip his hand back and take a deep breath and smile so wide.

I meet Joe's eyes one last time, then stand up *straight*, open my mouth and. . .

There's a really tinny screech from overhead.

"You don't understand, this *is* an *emergency*." I hear Aimee's voice from the tannoy, followed by a little cough, and then her voice rings out, clear as a bell.

"Introducing . . . Erin Woods!"

I wait for a second, because I'm not sure exactly what's going to happen next, but then the backing track for "Together" starts playing over the tannoy. I listen to the melody and I wait for my cue and I look down at Joe as he squeezes my hand and then I start singing.

I sing for Joe. I sing for Aimee. I sing for my family, and I sing for *me*.

I forget that anyone is watching me, and I put *everything* into that song. All of my frustrations, my fears, my hopes and my joy bursting out of my mouth and into the lyrics.

And then, as I reach the chorus, belting out the words, Shani, Robin and Brooke throw down their hoods and . . . *join in!*

There's a bit of a gasp in the airport and even more people flock over, because OMG, Fusion are performing right now in the airport!

I'm *singing with Fusion*.

We're smiling and holding hands, and this is quite possibly the very best moment of my entire life.

The backing track ends, and we stop singing.

I'm panting.

"Phffff." I exhale as I meet Shani's eyes. "Was that OK?"

"I'd say so!" Shani shakes her head as she leans down towards me. "That was great."

The tannoy music starts up again, and the next thing I hear is the song that I freestyled to from my audition video. The one called "September", by Earth, Wind & Fire.

I see Shani smile and turn to Brooke and Robin and whisper, "I love this song."

I meet Joe's eyes again as he backs up to the safety of Mum's legs and my foot starts tapping.

I've always told him that it's OK to be different. That it's OK to stand out.

My shoulders start to wiggle in time with the beat.

I've always told him that we should celebrate what's different about us.

I throw my arms wide, then start clapping my hands in time with the beat and grin *so* wide.

Mum and Joe start clapping too. Then Nanny, then Dad and Barbara. The people who are standing around watching start nodding their heads and gradually, they

273

start clapping too, even Shani, Robin and Brooke.

I am smiling and clapping and now my legs start moving and without even meaning to, I just start dancing. I forget that everyone is watching me, and I let myself move to the beat of the music, and next thing I know, Shani, Robin and Brooke are dancing with me, and then everyone starts dancing! Like we're at a disco or something!

It's completely surreal and a bit weird and completely and utterly *amazing*.

The music keeps playing over the tannoy and Aimee appears.

"I thought you'd left me!" I hug her tight.

"Never." She shimmies next to me. "But anyway, you've got this!" She opens her arms wide as we look at everyone dancing. "And we . . ." She points to herself, then my family, then Barbara and Pat, who seems to have appeared from nowhere. ". . . well, we've got *you*."

I don't know how long the music plays for. Definitely long enough for us all to dance to "Proud Mary" and "Kung Fu Fighting" and "Sweet Caroline", but after a short while the music stops, and a voice comes over the tannoy to remind everyone that it really is the last, last call for flight LAX9116.

"That was a great audition." Shani smiles down at me.

"Seriously cool."

"Thanks." I grin. Did Shani really just tell me that I'm cool?! No way!

"That was amazing, Erin!" Aimee throws her arms around me.

"Oh my goodness, Erin!" Mum hugs me. "I'm so proud of you!" She stands back and gives her tummy a little rub.

"Thanks, Mum." I put my hand over hers. "You know, I've been thinking about the new baby and how maybe it's nice that we're all so different. The new baby will be your only child who doesn't have achondroplasia, and I'm your only child who has brown skin and Joe's the only boy. So even though we all have things that we can share, we all have things that make us completely individual too."

"You're so right, Erin." Mum sidles towards me. "And you might all be different, but your dad and I love you all just the same." She squeezes my hand. "You're going to be an amazing older sister to the baby, you know?"

Dad wipes a tear from his eye.

"And Joe's going to make an amazing older brother." I watch Joe as he shows Shani some of his kung fu moves. He meets my gaze, spreads his arms wide and runs towards me.

But just before he reaches me, he loses his balance

and stumbles to the floor.

Everyone gasps and looks down at Joe in a heap.

It's his absolute worst nightmare.

Before I have a chance to help him, Joe stands back up. He dusts down his knees and looks at all of the people staring at him.

I watch his bottom lip, ready for it to tremble at any second.

It doesn't.

Instead, he looks at all of the onlookers, makes a really menacing face and shows them his best roundhouse kick.

There's a collective sigh of relief and everyone smiles and moves on.

"That was amazing, Joe." I beam. "Where did you learn to do that?" And I'm totally talking about the kick, but Joe stands back, looks me in the eye and says:

"You."

My cheeks glow with proper happiness. Because now I *know*, whatever happens next, this moment makes the last few weeks completely and totally worth it.

CHAPTER 37

Two Months Later

I can't believe that it's finally here.

The night that we've been counting down to ever since my audition with Fusion.

The most hotly anticipated concert in the whole of Belfast. A concert that sold out in eighteen seconds! A concert that I actually got *given* tickets for.

Fusion ... featuring ... *Fusion Junior!*

And here I am, stuck in my dressing room, trying to reach the lock with my left shoe.

"Is there anything that you can stand on?" Aimee calls from outside the door as I look back into the room with a sigh.

"Yes," I reply as I start pulling over a chair towards the

door. I unlock it and open it to see Aimee, Mum, Dad, Nanny and Joe smiling at me from the hallway.

We hear an excited cheer from the arena.

"Do you think that's Fusion going onstage?" Aimee turns towards the sound as this amazing drumbeat pounds out. It gets faster and faster and faster until all of a sudden it stops and everything goes quiet.

"Good evening, Belfast!" bursts out from the arena.

"I think it might be!" I nod with a grin.

"Well, we'd better go and take our seats." Mum gives me a hug as Dad and Nanny hover next to us. "We're really proud of you, you know?"

"Thanks, Mum." I lean in towards her.

"Good luck, Erin!" Joe throws his arms around my legs.

"You'll be grand, Erin." Nanny gives me a friendly pat on the arm.

"Do you want me to stay here with you?" Aimee asks as she meets my eyes.

"It's OK." I look nervously towards the stage door. "You shouldn't miss the concert."

"Don't be silly, Erin." Aimee's eyes sparkle. "I don't want to watch it without you. Well, not until you're in it anyway."

"Five minutes and we'll need you onstage." The lady from the airport says at the door. "They'll announce you after 'Love My Life', then you'll be singing 'Together' with them, OK?"

"Yep." I nod and try not to show how nervous I'm feeling.

"Good luck, Erin." Aimee puts her hand into a pocket and pulls out a mint humbug. "This is in case you get hungry." She passes it to me, just as Fusion start singing "Love My Life". She hugs me tight, then walks out to take her seat in the audience.

I hum along to "Love My Life" as I follow the lady from the airport into the wings of the stage, where two other girls are standing waiting, and we all smile at each other shyly.

"Listen up, Belfast!" Shani calls out.

The whole arena goes *deathly* quiet.

"Tonight, you get to watch the debut performance of three very important people," Brooke is speaking now.

"Tonight, we'd like to introduce you to..." Robin pauses as everyone waits.

"*Fusion Junior!*" they all shout together, and the audience goes completely *wild*.

I take a deep breath. This is it. I've got this.

"Come out here, girls." Shani beckons us on to the stage. "Everyone's dying to meet you!"

I take a deep breath, a huge beaming smile filling my face, and I walk out into the bright lights of the stage.

ACKNOWLEDGEMENTS

Writing this book has been a huge team effort. We've worked together as co-authors, but we've also been supported, guided and encouraged by so many others!
We would both like to thank the following people:

Our fabulous agent, Kate Shaw. Thank you so much for your guidance, your belief and for laughing in all the right places. You're the best.

Our awesome editor, Linas Alsenas. This book simply wouldn't be here without you! Thank you so much for bringing us together on this amazing project. For your vision, your encouragement and your warmth and humour. You have been a beacon throughout.

The whole talented (and also super lovely) team at Scholastic, who have put together such an amazing bundle of fun in this book! Especially Jessica White for her great copyediting, Sarah Dutton, who has been so lovely to work with polishing the text, our publicist Emily Burns and marketing legend Ella Probert. Thanks also to Liam Drane for the incredible front cover.

Special thanks to Cathy Reay for her valuable, insightful feedback on issues of representation throughout the book.

Chrissie would like to thank all of her brilliant friends and fellow writers (especially her Golden Egg buddies) for all of the encouragement, humour and patience. Special thanks to Kate Perry who has been quite possibly the best cheerleader EVER. And of course, her family – who all give so much support and love. Most importantly, her husband Rich and their two children, Meg and Hattie. For the coffees, the homemade cakes, the reminders to take a break and the unlimited hugs. Best. Team. Ever.

Cara would like to thank her mum and dad for listening to and believing in all of her crazy ideas. Noah and Bethany, the best brother and sister, who make her laugh every day! Her nanny, for the shopping and coffee trips to Forestside; for never saying "that's too big" or "they're too long" and getting the scissors and sewing machine out to help her rock any look! To her friends for the giggles, the dance routines and the TikToks along the way! A special shout out to all the staff, teachers and classroom assistants at St Joseph's PS and Assumption Grammar, for never being a Barbara and helping her learn and grow in her unique way!!

Last but by no means least, to anyone reading this: being different can be hard sometimes, but remember you're amazing and keep telling yourself, "I got this!"

ABOUT THE AUTHORS

Cara Mailey lives in Belfast with her family, who were all featured in BBC One's "Keeping Up With the Maileys". Cara first gained notice when she appeared on CBBC "The Dengineers". "My Life: Made to Measure" was a CBBC documentary that followed the development of "She's Fierce By Cara", her fashion line for girls with achondroplasia, created in partnership with Amanda Rabour and TJ Hannif.

Chrissie Sains lives in Essex with her husband and two children. She is the author of several books, including *An Alien in the Jam Factory* and *The Treasure Under the Jam Factory*.